SO-ATA-942

JAN 0 6

DATE DUE

4 25 04			
JUN 5 '06			
AUG 1			
JAN 03 08			
1/22/08			
GAYLORD			PRINTED IN U.S.A.

ALASKA:
Iditarod Dream
and
Christmas Dream

*Also by Tracie Peterson
in Large Print:*

Alaska: Destiny's Road
Alaska: A Light in the Window
Beneath a Harvest Sky
Across the Years
Shadows of the Canyon
The Long-Awaited Child
Controlling Interests
Framed

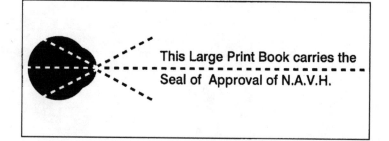

This Large Print Book carries the
Seal of Approval of N.A.V.H.

ALASKA:
Iditarod Dream
and
Christmas Dream

*Two Inspirational Love Stories
from America's Final Frontier*

Tracie Peterson

Thorndike Press • Waterville, Maine

JACKSON COUNTY LIBRARY SERVICES
MEDFORD OREGON 97501

Iditarod Dream copyright © 1994 by Tracie J. Peterson.
Christmas Dream copyright © 1996 by Barbour Publishing, Inc.

Scripture references in *Iditarod Dream* are taken from the
HOLY BIBLE: NEW INTERNATIONAL VERSION®. Copyright
1973, 1978, 1984 by International Bible Society. Used by
permission of Zondervan Publishing House. All rights
reserved.

All rights reserved.

Published in 2005 by arrangement with
Barbour Publishing, Inc.

Thorndike Press® Large Print Christian Fiction.

The tree indicium is a trademark of Thorndike Press.

The text of this Large Print edition is unabridged.
Other aspects of the book may vary from the original edition.

Set in 16 pt. Plantin by Liana M. Walker.

Printed in the United States on permanent paper.

Library of Congress Cataloging-in-Publication Data

Peterson, Tracie.
    Alaska : Iditarod dream and Christmas dream :
  two inspirational love stories from America's final
  frontier / by Tracie Peterson. — Large print ed.
    p. cm. — (Thorndike Press large print Christian fiction)
  Iditarod dream originally published: Waterville : Barbour
Pub., 1994; Christmas dream originally published:
Waterville : Barbour Pub., 1996.
    ISBN 0-7862-8133-2 (lg. print : hc : alk. paper)
    1. Iditarod (Race) — Fiction.   2. Alaska — Fiction.
3. Large type books.   I. Peterson, Tracie. Iditarod dream.
II. Peterson, Tracie. Christmas dream.   III. Title.
IV. Thorndike Press large print Christian fiction series.
PS3566.E7717A793 2005
  813'.54—dc22   2005022153

Dedication

To Pam and David, Cheri,
and Ryan Thibault.

To Joyce and Ray Mains,
my personal Alaska connection.

Thanks for your love
and prayers over the years.
I thank God upon my
every remembrance of you.

National Association for Visually Handicapped
---------------------------------- *serving the partially seeing*

As the Founder/CEO of NAVH, the only national health agency solely devoted to those who, although not totally blind, have an eye disease which could lead to serious visual impairment, I am pleased to recognize Thorndike Press* as one of the leading publishers in the large print field.

Founded in 1954 in San Francisco to prepare large print textbooks for partially seeing children, NAVH became the pioneer and standard setting agency in the preparation of large type.

Today, those publishers who meet our standards carry the prestigious "Seal of Approval" indicating high quality large print. We are delighted that Thorndike Press is one of the publishers whose titles meet these standards. We are also pleased to recognize the significant contribution Thorndike Press is making in this important and growing field.

Lorraine H. Marchi, L.H.D.
Founder/CEO
NAVH

* Thorndike Press encompasses the following imprints: Thorndike, Wheeler, Walker and Large Print Press.

Iditarod
Dream

Chapter 1

Rita Eriksson shifted into overdrive and watched the highway miles pass by in disinterested silence. Although she'd been away from her childhood home for over five years, the idea of returning held little interest for her.

Born Rita Anne Eriksson, she was the last of ten children and the least cut out for rural life. At least that's what she told herself when she left for college and a degree in nursing.

She'd spent the better part of a lifetime living forty minutes outside the small town of Tok, Alaska. A town seemingly misplaced in the middle of nowhere, between Fairbanks and the Canadian border. Its claim to fame was dogsledding and touristy native art, but to Rita, its only appeal was the fact that the Alcan Highway ran through it. It was on that highway, shortly after she'd finished school, that Rita took off for Anchorage and never looked back.

Ignoring the speed of her car, Rita gave anxious thought to her return home. Most of her brothers and sisters had moved away from Tok, although an older brother and his family had settled in town. Her family was seemingly scattered to the four winds, and for Rita, it was just as well. She'd never fit in with any of them and had come along too late for most of them to even bother being interested in her. Her closest sibling, Edgar, was nearly nine years her senior and, being a boy, he had little interest in the surprise arrival of another sister.

Rita had been only too happy to escape the mundane lifestyle of a home that, until recently, hadn't even afforded them the luxury of electricity or an indoor bathroom. It might not have been so bad had they lived in town. In comparison to the desolation of the Eriksson homestead, there were many things to do in Tok. But Rita had decided to put it all behind her and be done with that way of life.

Yet, even though that had been her choice, here she was driving back home at her parents' urging. Well, not really her parents' urging, more like her father's. She'd always felt closer to her father. For reasons that were beyond Rita's understanding, she and her mother had never gotten along. It seemed that no matter how hard Rita tried, her relationship with her mother only deteriorated to the point that neither of them put much effort into mending the emotional cavern.

Her father, however, loved her, and of that Rita was certain. He never failed to call her on Monday nights to find out how her weekend had gone and how the week to come was shaping up. During the entire five years in Anchorage, Rita could remember her mother calling only twice and both those times were on Christmas.

With a shake of her head, Rita tried to ignore the pain she still felt whenever she thought of her mother. There was no sense in letting the past get a stronghold, Rita determined. Nothing was going to change between them. Hadn't time already proved that?

She didn't know how long the flashing red lights of the patrol car had followed her, but when the officer behind the wheel hit the blaring sirens, Rita nearly jumped out of her skin.

"Oh, no!" she muttered and pulled the

car to the side of the road. "I wonder how fast I was going?"

She rolled down the window and ran a hand through her newly cropped black hair. This trip was turning sour rather soon, she thought to herself.

"May I see your driver's license?" a voice called out from overhead.

Rita didn't even bother to look up. She reached over for her red clutch purse and produced her license. Without a word, she handed the license over and then sat tapping her fingers against the steering wheel.

"You were doing eighty-five miles an hour, Ms. Eriksson. Say, you wouldn't be related to August and Beth Eriksson?" the officer questioned.

Rita perked up. Maybe she could beat the ticket if she turned on a little hometown charm.

"Why, yes. They're my parents," she said with a honey-smooth voice. Glancing up behind thick black lashes, Rita offered a smile to the stout-looking patrolman whose name tag read "Williams."

The officer took off his sunglasses and returned Rita's smile. "Good friends of mine, your folks. I doubt they'd enjoy burying one of their own," he stated evenly. "Being a native, you know better than to drive that fast on this highway. If the road doesn't tear up your vehicle, wrapping it around a moose or grizzly sure could do the job."

"Sorry," Rita said, trying hard to maintain her temper. She didn't appreciate being told what she should and shouldn't do.

"I would hope for at least that much," the officer said as he returned Rita's license with a ticket attached. "I'd let you off with a warning, but being you're a native and not all that sorry, I'd just as soon you learn a lesson."

Rita's temper got the best of her as she snatched the ticket and license from his hand. She thought to say something, but instead stuffed the items inside her purse and turned to roll up her window.

"It was a pleasure meeting you, Ms. Eriksson. I'm sure we'll be seeing more of each other. By the way, I'm Mark Williams."

"It wasn't a pleasure meeting you, Officer Williams, and I hope we don't meet again," Rita said curtly and rolled up the car window. She barely waited for the man to walk past her car before hitting the gas and spraying gravel behind her as she pulled back up on the highway.

Rita watched uncomfortably for any sign that the patrol car intended to follow her. When it remained in place at the side of the highway, she breathed a sigh of relief and glanced at her watch.

She'd already been driving for four hours without stopping to get out and stretch, and her legs and some other body parts were beginning to ache.

She calculated that her destination was still another hour away. Making mental note of the scenery and the mile markers, Rita realized there wouldn't be much in the way of places to take a break, and when the first available turn off the highway presented itself, she took it.

Bouncing down the dusty gravel road, Rita found herself coming to a stop when the road dead-ended. Grimacing, Rita walked several yards into the trees and decided to walk a little farther and stretch her legs.

Tall, black spruce rose up in contrast against the long, white trunks of birch trees, while the lavender petals of fireweed waved welcomes from their red stems.

Rita pushed on through the trees and underbrush, enjoying the walk in spite of herself. Something about the area seemed more than just vaguely familiar and, when the trees gave way to a small lake, Rita recognized the place as one she and her father had dogsledded to on many occasions.

The very thought of dogsledding caused Rita to smile. If the truth were known, it was the main reason she'd allowed her father to talk her into coming back home for a visit. He was trying to help her dream of racing in the Iditarod come true.

The Iditarod! A dogsled race to equal no other and Rita was determined to one day be a part of it. She still remembered stories her father had told her about the old dogsled mail trails. Moonlit nights on the trail, the icy winds, and the solitude of having nothing and no one but yourself and the dogs against the elements. It thrilled Rita like nothing else and she wouldn't be complete until she'd experienced "The Last Great Race."

"Ooof!"

The sound caused the hair to prickle on the back of Rita's neck. Snapping her head up, she searched the area for the unmistakable sound of a disturbed bear.

No more than twenty feet away, a mother grizzly woofed a command to her cub before striking a protective stance between Rita and her young.

Rita knew better than to run or cry.

15

Bears seemed more inclined to attack humans when they made noises similar to animals in distress. August had told his daughter on more than one occasion to stand her ground silently and only as a last resort should she curl up into a ball and play dead.

Rita shoved her hands into the pockets of her fleece-lined sweattop and made eye contact with the grizzly. The bear took a step forward and made a grunting woof.

Rita could feel her legs trembling beneath her jeans. She knew she was in grave danger, but there was nothing to do but wait out the situation. Somewhere to her left, Rita heard a rustling in the brush. Would it be another bear? Perhaps the cub had somehow gotten behind her.

The bear advanced another two steps at the same time Mark Williams emerged from the trees. Rita's relief was short-lived, however, as the mother bear let out a roar.

"Don't move," Mark said in a hushed tone.

"Don't worry," Rita breathed, "I won't."

Rita struggled to keep from going back on her word. Her fear told her to run, and yet her mind rationalized that it would be exactly the wrong thing to do.

"Give her your jacket," Mark suggested.

"What?" Rita questioned in a whisper.

"Take off your jacket and toss it on the ground. Move real slow and don't throw it at her, just over in that direction," Mark said, while slowly pulling his revolver from its holster.

Rita slowly pulled her hands from her pockets. "But it's not a jacket," Rita argued under her breath.

"I don't care if it's a ball gown. Just give it to her and maybe she'll be satisfied enough to let you back away. If not," Mark leveled the .44 magnum in the direction of the bear, "I'll shoot and you back away."

Rita contemplated his words for only a moment before reaching up to undo the zipper. Making deliberate, slow moves, Rita eased out of her top and tossed it to the side of the grizzly.

"Now, move away," Mark said as he put himself between Rita and the bear.

The bear grunted and stomped at her shirt while Rita and Mark backed away. The bear clamped mighty jaws around the fabric of Rita's top and trotted off in the direction the cub had disappeared. When she was out of sight, Mark stopped and put a hand on Rita's arm.

"Are you all right?" he questioned.

Rita suddenly became conscious of

being cold, wearing a thin, form-fitting tank top.

Mark tried to hide a grin while he eased out of his jacket. "Here, I wouldn't want you to catch a chill."

Rita couldn't bear the humiliation and grabbed the jacket without a word. She pulled it on while walking back to her car.

"I have more clothes in the car," she called over her shoulder. "I'll give this back to you in a minute."

"What, no thanks?" Mark questioned in a teasing tone.

Rita refused to give in to his bantering. "I was doing okay," she said, fumbling in her jeans for her car keys.

"Oh, yeah, I could see that," Mark replied sarcastically.

Rita opened the trunk and pulled out a suitcase. Grabbing the first thing she could find, Rita produced an ecru-colored sweater, which she put on.

"There," Rita said as she threw the jacket against Mark's back. "Now that you've done your good deed for the day you can go."

Mark turned around and picked up his patrol jacket. "Is there some reason you can't be civil?" His tone of voice told

Rita he wasn't kidding.

She stared for a moment at the brown-haired man. His dark eyes seemed to pierce her conscience. "Sorry," she offered by way of an apology.

"Well, that's at least civil," Mark said as he pulled his jacket back on. "Look, I'm mighty fond of your father and mother, and I know it'd pretty much break their hearts if you were to get yourself killed."

"Don't worry about it," Rita said, reverting to her anger. "*I* don't."

"What's with you?" Mark questioned the angry, petite woman.

"I don't see that my private life is any of your business. This whole situation has been more than a little embarrassing and now, if you'll excuse me, I'm expected at home," Rita stormed the words and climbed into her car.

"Don't speed," Mark said with a grin.

Rita felt more frustration than she was willing to put into words. She flashed her dark eyes at Mark. "Like I said, don't worry about it. I'm a big girl."

"I'm well aware of that, Ms. Eriksson," Mark offered with a chuckle. "I'm very well aware of that."

Chapter 2

"We're mighty glad to see you home safe," August Eriksson said, embracing Rita.

Rita nearly fell into her father's arms. How she longed for a human touch, although she would have never admitted it. "It's good to see you, Dad," Rita whispered against his ear. She pulled back and scrutinized the man before her. He seemed so much older than she remembered. His hair was snowy white and his face much more wrinkled and worn.

Beth Ericksson emerged from the kitchen to appraise the scene. "Hello, Rita," she offered with a smile. "Good to have you back."

"Thanks, Mom," Rita replied and went to where her mother stood. The embrace they shared wasn't the same as the one Rita had just given her father. It was curt, almost a polite symbolic gesture.

"Are you hungry?" Beth asked her daughter.

"Starved and then some," Rita answered with a laugh. "I didn't plan on taking so long to get here."

"Well, I have some sandwich makings in the kitchen. Why don't you just leave your things until after you eat. Then you can get settled in your old room," her mother said in an unemotional way. From the tone set between mother and daughter, it would have been impossible to tell that they were anything more than acquaintances. And, in Rita's mind, they were merely that and little more.

Rita followed her mother and father into the kitchen. They seemed as happy with one another as they had when she was a child. Her father still looked at her mother with a glow of admiration in his eyes. What was it that he saw in her that merited such praise?

Rita sat politely listening as her parents filled her in on the community and all that had happened in five years. She hung on her father's every word, while barely commenting on her mother's information regarding the family.

"And so, have you considered what I suggested?" August asked.

"And what was that, dear?" Beth asked with a note of surprise in her voice.

"I suggested that our daughter take time off before joining the work force grind and race the Iditarod next year," August answered his wife.

Beth's face masked any reaction she had to August's words and instead she simply replied, "How interesting."

Rita wondered how her mother really felt about the matter. Would she resent her youngest daughter's presence in the big, rambling log home?

"I have been thinking about it," Rita admitted. "I know the opportunity is one that will probably never come again."

"That's why you should jump at the chance," her father remarked.

"I'm so out of shape, though. What with all my studies and work at the hospital, I haven't been outdoors long enough to walk around the block. I can only imagine what it would be like to run with a dogsled team," Rita replied, taking the plate her mother offered. Despite their differences, Rita noted that her mother had made her favorite, roast beef sandwiches.

"Thanks, Mom," Rita added and offered her mother a hint of a smile.

"But all of that will come back to you.

You can start this summer and run with the dogs. You can spend all fall and winter on the trails around here, maybe even run in another race or two just to get primed for the big one," August said in a way that almost sounded as though he were begging.

"And you really think I'd be able to do it?" Rita asked, hopefully. "You think I could manage it all? All the training and getting into shape?"

"You're no Eriksson if you can't!" August exclaimed good-naturedly. "Besides, you'll have nine months to do it in. I've got plenty of good dogs and there's a friend or two in the area that would be happy to have you along on practice runs."

"What do you mean? You'd be handling my training, wouldn't you?" Rita inquired.

"Now, Rita, I'm not the young man I used to be. I can't handle the trails like before. I'll take care of things around here, but when you start practicing on the rougher trails, you'll have to do it without me," August answered.

"But being with you was the biggest reason I was considering it," Rita said in a pouting tone.

"Rita," Beth said a little harsher than she'd intended, "your father is entitled to

23

take care of himself. I need him as much as you do."

Rita turned to face her mother for a moment. There was no need in sharing their differences only twenty minutes into their visit. "I understand that, Mother. I guess if I do it, I'll just run alone."

"There's really no need to do that. Like I said, I have a couple of trusted friends in the area and you could learn a lot from them. Especially where the newer techniques come into play. Both of them even raced in the Iditarod last year. They know a whole heap more about what to expect than I do. You know very well that my only attempt was several years ago and I didn't even finish the race."

"Yes, but you won the silver ingots for being the first to reach the halfway point," Rita offered as consolation.

"I know, but I dropped out shortly after that and these men have both completed the race. Besides, I trust them completely and I know you'd like them. They'd make interesting company and maybe you'd even find yourself fancying one of them. They're both single."

"Oh, Dad," Rita moaned and rolled her eyes. "I'm certainly not up here to husband hunt."

"Then what are you up here for? You haven't seen us in over five years and yet I know that it wasn't for the joy of seeing us that you came home. You want that race. You've always wanted it. Are you going to throw away the only chance you may ever have to race the Iditarod? Are you going to give up your dream?" August asked seriously.

Rita contemplated her father's words for a moment. She was grateful that her mother remained silent. Her father was perfectly right about the conditions being too hard for him. He wasn't young anymore, and yet Rita really needed him to be.

"All right," Rita finally spoke. "I'll go for it. I'll do it your way and I'll finish the race for both of us!"

"Good girl," August said, slamming his hands down on the table. "By next March you'll be able to run with the pros and I'll expect a healthy finish."

"What? You don't demand that I win?" Rita said with a laugh.

"No, it'll be enough just to see you run it and do your best," August replied with pride beaming in his eyes. None of his other children had taken the interest in dogsledding that Rita had, and he was excited about her decision.

Rita turned to her mother. Beth sat quietly eating her sandwich, her face void of anything that would signal to Rita what she thought of the plan.

"Will it be all right with you, Mom?" Rita dared the question.

Beth looked surprised that Rita would consult her about her feelings on the matter. "I support whatever your father wants, Rita. I, too, hope to see you accomplish your dream. It won't be an easy task, but then good things seldom come free of strife."

Rita nodded. "I guess when I'm done here, I'll unpack my things. Then you can tell me where we go from there, Dad."

"Oh, I nearly forgot," August remarked with a quick glance at his wife, "we've planned a bit of a homecoming party for you."

"I wish you hadn't," Rita said, with noted frustration in her voice. "You know how I hate parties."

"That's what I told him, but he insisted," Beth offered.

"Well," August continued, "it's just a small get-together. Old friends, new friends, maybe even some family. Tonight at seven, and I promise not to throw another one without consulting you first."

His eyes betrayed the anticipation of showing his youngest daughter off, and so Rita agreed without fuss.

I only have to get through this evening, Rita thought as she ate her sandwich. *After that everything else will be simple.*

Rita tried on three outfits before finally settling on a calf-length denim skirt and light-blue cashmere sweater. She was finishing dressing by pulling on high, black boots when a knock sounded at the door.

"It's open," Rita called out as she finished with her boots.

"Are you nearly ready?" Beth asked her daughter. She noted how graceful Rita looked as she crossed the room and ran a brush through her short, dark hair. She was so much like her father.

"Just finishing up," Rita replied over her shoulder. "I couldn't decide what to wear."

"You look fine," Beth offered, hoping that it wouldn't offend Rita. Sometimes the strangest things seemed to set her daughter off.

"You really think so?" Rita asked, running a hand down her skirt. "Everything seemed wrinkled."

"It looks nice, Rita. Your father is really anxious to show you off, and since most everyone is already here, I thought I'd escort you. That is, if you don't mind," Beth stated hopefully.

Rita was surprised at her mother's gesture but refused to show it. "It sounds fine, Mom," she said, following her mother into the hall.

Descending the stairs, Rita could hear the soft, classical music her mother had put on the stereo. Mozart. No, Chopin, Rita decided. It sounded nice, and Rita turned to tell Beth so but found her mother's attention already directed to the crowd as they stepped into the vestibule.

"Beth, don't you look pretty," an older man said as he stepped forward and kissed Rita's mother on the cheek.

"You're kind to say so, Ernie, but I think you'd best have the eye doctor check out your vision," Beth replied and Ernie laughed. "Rita, you remember Ernie, don't you?"

"Of course," Rita said and smiled sweetly.

"Well, don't be telling me this is the baby of the family," Ernie replied, giving Rita a hearty squeeze. "It don't seem possible."

"I know what you mean," August said as

he came up from behind Beth. "Rita's become a nurse just like her aunt Julie. I can't believe a person could change so much in just five years."

"I grew up, Daddy," Rita offered. "That's all. Are you still in the kennel business, Ernie?" Rita hoped her question would take the focus off of herself. She remembered Ernie loved to talk about his dogs.

"Naw, gave it up about a year ago. Got to be too much work for just me," Ernie replied.

"Boy, that's the truth," August said, sounding tired. "That's why I got a partner. None of the kids seemed interested in joining me, so it seemed the logical thing to do."

"A partner?" Rita questioned her father in surprise. "When did you get a partner?"

August chuckled at Rita's reaction. "I guess I forgot to tell you about that. I'll introduce you to him tonight. He's a real nice guy, and one of those fellows I was telling you about earlier."

Rita bit back a response as her mother pulled her along and into a sea of people. "I thought you said this was a *small* get-together," Rita commented.

"To your father, this *is* a small get-together," Beth reminded her daughter.

Rita nodded, knowing how her father loved to keep friends and family close at hand. He was always inviting someone over for some reason.

"Rita!" a woman's voice exclaimed.

Rita looked up to find an old high school friend. "Janice?"

She barely resembled the girl Rita had known. Her once-long blond hair was cut short, and her figure was generously rounded in the expectation of a new child.

"It's really me," the woman replied. "I can't believe you're finally here. You will come over to spend some time with me and Dave, won't you?"

"Of course," Rita said, still stunned by her friend's appearance.

"We're living in Tok, same old place, so just make your way on over whenever you can. But I warn you, the place is a mess, what with the kids and all," Janice said with a laugh.

"Kids? I thought maybe this was your first one," Rita said, indicating Janice's condition.

"Oh, no. This is number five," Janice replied.

"Five?" Rita questioned. She could see that Janice was radiant and happy and knew there wasn't any sense in spoiling it with lectures of world conditions and such. "How nice," Rita added instead and left the woman with promises to visit.

She made the rounds bidding "hellos" to all the neighbors and church friends that she'd known. That life seemed a million years ago, however, and Rita felt rather out of place. So many of these people had drifted out of her thoughts and heart, and now she felt hesitant to allow them back in.

Independence had made Rita hard. She knew it and she actually found herself supporting the role. Being aloof and indifferent left her more time to herself and with more control in her life.

She was just trying to figure a way out of the room when August called from the doorway. "Rita, come meet my partner."

Rita made her way through the crowd of well-wishers and glanced up in time to come face-to-face with Mark Williams.

"Rita, this is Mark Williams, my partner," August stated. "Mark, my youngest daughter, Rita."

Mark grinned from ear to ear and extended his hand. "Rita, it's a pleasure."

"I don't believe this," Rita said, refusing Mark's hand and turning to her father.

"*He's* your partner?"

"Do you two know each other?" August asked, looking curiously from Mark to Rita.

"You'll have to excuse me," Rita said, and hurried from the room.

She hated herself for the way she'd responded to Mark's presence, but she couldn't imagine anything more embarrassing than having to face Mark Williams again. Making her way through the kitchen and out the back door, Rita didn't stop moving until she was well behind the house and halfway to the creek that ran the full length of the property.

"I don't believe it," she sighed aloud. "It's bad enough Dad's taken on a partner, but why did it have to be him?"

The breeze picked up, chilling Rita momentarily. She hugged her arms to her chest and gazed up into the sky.

"You really should learn to layer your clothes," Mark teased.

Rita snapped around to find him not two feet from where she stood. "Haven't you put me through enough? First you give me a speeding ticket, then you make me give up my clothes to a bear, and now I learn that I must endure your company for the months to come if I'm to get the training I need for the Iditarod."

"In the first place, you deserved the speeding ticket," Mark said with a shrug. "Now, are you going to dispute that?"

"No, I suppose not," Rita muttered.

"And secondly, as embarrassing as it was, giving your top to that grizzly got her attention on something other than you, and finally, I told you that your folks and I were good friends," Mark stated firmly.

"Good friends are one thing. Partners are entirely something else. I had no idea my father had even taken on a partner, much less that it was you," Rita said, and turned to walk away.

"I wish for the sake of your father and mother, you'd just drop what's gone behind us. I'd like to start over," Mark said, following Rita back to the house.

Rita stopped and turned to face the man who'd caused her nothing but embarrassment and grief. "Look, for my father's sake I will act civilly and cooperate. But, and this is most important," Rita said with determination, "I don't need you or anyone else telling me how to live my life. I can take care of myself, just as I have for the last five years. I came here to train for the Iditarod, not to make friends or hunt for a husband, as my father would like me to do."

"I can't imagine wanting to be either one," Mark replied sarcastically and left Rita to stare open-mouthed after him.

Chapter 3

At breakfast the following morning, Rita was still thinking about Mark's words. She wasn't sure why it should bother her so much, but it did.

He had no right to talk to me that way, Rita thought. She shoveled scrambled eggs and toast into her mouth without even tasting the food.

"You're kind of preoccupied this morning, aren't you?" August asked his daughter and took a seat beside her.

"Sorry," Rita offered, wiping toast crumbs from her tee-shirt. "I just keep thinking about all the work I need to do." It wasn't a lie, Rita decided. She really had been thinking of a variety of things. It was just that Mark Williams seemed to take up most of her attention.

"Well, I think the first thing we do should be to reacquaint you with the dogs.

There's a few of the older ones we use for breeding who'll remember you, but the dogs you'll need to use for the race will be the three- and four-year-old ones."

"I thought of that," Rita said, sipping hot coffee. "I can do the feeding and care for the ones you pick out."

"We'll work together to pick out twenty or thirty that look like good possibilities for the race. You can work with those dogs on a daily basis," August stated. "We can choose them after breakfast, if that's all right with you."

"Sounds good to me," Rita replied. She looked forward to working with her father and, in spite of her worries about his health and age, Rita knew the kennel was his domain.

Half an hour later, Rita followed her father from dog to dog. The Eriksson kennel had over one hundred dogs, far more animals than had been there before Rita had gone to Anchorage. It was easy to see why August needed a partner.

After only ten minutes of listening to her father point out the virtues of one dog after the other, Rita was annoyed to find herself having to deal with Mark again.

"Good morning," Mark said as he

passed by with a bag of feed hoisted over his shoulder.

"It was," Rita muttered and turned to her father. "What's he doing here?"

"I told you. He's my partner. One hundred and ten dogs need a lot of attention. We work at this thing on a constant basis," August replied.

"But I thought he was a cop," Rita said without thinking her father might wonder how she knew that detail of Mark's life.

"Oh, that," August said with a shrug. "He just fills in on the weekends. Most of the time he's here with me."

"Great," Rita stated sarcastically and walked away to look at the dogs on her own.

"There's a lot of anger in that woman," Mark stated, putting the feed on the ground beside him. He pulled out a ball cap from his back pocket and secured it on his head.

"I know," August replied. He watched as Rita moved from dog to dog. She'd always gotten along better with animals than people, August reminded himself. It wouldn't have been all that surprising had she handled Mark with cool indifference, but her hateful attitude seemed out of place, even for Rita.

August turned to Mark. "What happened between you two? She has a real mean streak for you."

Mark chuckled and relayed his first and second meeting with Rita. He finished up by telling August about their conversation the night of the party.

"I guess she thought she was losing control of the situation. Control has always been a big issue with Rita." August's words caused Mark to sober considerably.

"She won't have as much control out there on the trails. The weather, the wildlife, all of it has a mind of its own," Mark stated as if August didn't already know it.

"Rita's always cherished independence," August replied. He was still watching Rita and knew she was trying not to notice Mark and August as they talked. "Since she was a little girl, Rita has alienated herself from just about everything for fear it might require she give up some form of control in her life. Didn't matter what or who it was. She put up a wall between herself and her mother, God, teachers, friends, and sometimes even me."

"I wonder why she feels so insecure?" Mark questioned.

"Insecure? I've thought of Rita as a lot of things but never insecure. Why, she trekked out of here on her own as fast as her car could take her. Of course you know how she is behind the wheel," August added with a laugh.

Mark smiled, but he challenged August's words. "Rita strikes me as the type of person who's never found her niche. She seems out of place and I think she purposefully makes it that way in order that no one and nothing get too close. I think she's insecure about forming relationships. Maybe she's afraid that the feelings she puts out won't be reciprocated."

"I suppose that's a possibility. I just never thought about it. Now that I do, it seems to make some sense. I just always thought she was spoiled and headstrong."

"Oh she is that, August," Mark agreed. "But I don't think it's the reason she distances herself. No, I think Rita's been hurt by someone, and she's not about to let anyone have the chance to let her down again."

August grimaced at Mark's words. He knew only too well of the soured relationship between Rita and Beth. Rita had turned away from her mother at a very early age, but for what reason, August was never sure. Beth had never wanted to discuss it, and Rita claimed to never understand it. August had been forced to stand by helplessly while the relationship deteriorated at a rapid pace.

"Dad!" Rita called from the dogs. "Is this dog one of Blueberry's pups?"

August smiled. Blueberry had been Rita's favorite pet before she'd left for Anchorage. "You've got a good eye, Rita. That's Dandelion, so named because he used to chew on them all the time. He's a good runner and one of the very dogs I thought you could use."

Rita ran her hand over the husky's backside. "He feels real firm," she replied.

"And he's a great leader," Mark added. He and August walked to where Rita continued to check him out. "I've run him in lead just about every time I've had him out. He seems to get out of sorts if you do otherwise."

"I know the feeling," Rita muttered under her breath. Mark caught the words but said nothing.

"Look, Rita," August began, "I want you and Mark to work well together. Do you suppose you could put whatever is bothering you aside and just try to make the relationship work?"

Rita's head snapped up. She bit off a rhetorical reply when she saw the pleading in her father's eyes. He was the only man for which she'd even consider backing away from a fight.

Mark noticed the change in Rita's facial expression as she caught sight of her father. She truly loved the man, which gave Mark hope. At least she was capable of love. Now, why did that matter? Mark tossed the thought from his mind and waited for Rita to make some formal statement of peace.

Rita struggled for the right words. She didn't like giving in or letting Mark win, but for some reason it was important to her father and that made it important to her. "I'm sorry, Mark," Rita finally said, turning to face her adversary. "I guess I got carried away with my anger. Truce?"

"Truce," Mark said and offered his hand.

Rita reached out and took Mark's hand. She was instantly aware of the way his big hand engulfed her smaller one. It was difficult to allow the contact and yet almost pleasant the way he squeezed her hand and smiled.

Rita quickly dropped his hand, confused by the feelings Mark had stirred. "So what dogs do you recommend, Mark?" she quickly asked to cover up her feelings.

By late in the afternoon, Mark, Rita, and August had picked twenty-two dogs that seemed to fit the description of what Rita needed. These dogs had endurance and youth, experience and grace. They were a sturdy breed of husky, with crystal blue eyes and stout, firm bodies.

Rita worked with the men to relocate the dogs. They moved dog houses, straw, stake-out chains, and dogs, until Beth called them for supper.

"Have dinner with us, Mark," August said, walking with Rita to the outdoor pump.

"Naw," Mark said, pulling off the ball cap and stuffing it into his back pocket again. "I've got things to take care of at home. Besides, I threw a roast in the crockpot before I left this morning."

Rita was relieved at Mark's reply but said nothing. She pushed and pulled at the pump handle until icy water flowed in a steady stream. Washing her hands and face with the strong, disinfectant soap that was left on a metal stand beside the pump, Rita felt refreshed and famished.

The days that followed found Rita in a constant state of retraining. Things she'd learned as a child had to be reviewed, while new ideas and techniques were introduced.

Rita had taken to jogging with Dandelion, whom she immediately dubbed "Dandy." She wanted to establish a strong relationship with the dog before working with the others. If the leader and driver were to work as one, they had to know each other intimately.

Rita enjoyed the playful dog. He was easy to love and filled a void in Rita's heart. No wonder she'd always found the dogs such pleasant company. They didn't ask about your feelings but simply accepted whatever you were capable of giving.

One crisp morning as she finished her run with Dandy, Rita was surprised when Mark appeared on the gravel road astride a motorcycle.

"Morning," he called out as he came up alongside Rita and Dandy.

"Hi," Rita said and slowed to a rapid walk.

"Want a ride back?" Mark offered.

"No, I'm fine," Rita replied, trying to soften the severity of her tone. "I need to walk. I still have flappy legs and no muscle tone."

"You look pretty good to me," Mark said with a grin.

Rita blushed and tried to ignore the fact that Mark noticed her discomfort with a broader smile.

"Dad tells me that you're going to race in the Iditarod," Rita said, hoping to steer the conversation away from herself.

"That's right," Mark replied, keeping even pace with Rita.

"I wouldn't miss it. Last year I came in high enough to make money on it. I intend to win it this year."

"Oh, really?" Rita said as her eyes met Mark's.

"Do I denote a bit of challenge in that question?" Mark asked.

"You might," Rita said, enjoying the banter.

"You realize the odds are against you. Few women even race the Iditarod, much less win it. Besides, I'm more experienced than you and you have flappy legs. Remember?" Mark's amusement was contagious.

Rita smiled in spite of her resolve to be serious. "I thought you said they looked pretty good," Rita answered.

"They do, but not for dogsledding. I think they'd look great beneath the hem of a skirt while accompanying me to dinner." Mark's statement was a clear invitation.

Rita shook her head. "I'm not about to fraternize with the competition," she replied. "You might learn all my strategies, and then I'd lose the race to you."

"You will anyway," Mark said with a laugh. "And I already know all your strategies. I'm the teacher, remember?"

Rita tossed her head and ignored the laughing man at her side. She didn't like the way he made her feel. She was afraid of feeling too much for him and determined within herself to avoid a deeper relationship than that of student and teacher.

Later that night, Rita took a quiet moment for herself and walked down to see her dogs. They were a good bunch. Dandy was white and tawny brown with streaks of black. Muffin was black and white, while Raven was so named for her coal-black coat. Toby and Teddy were matched with white blazes against silver and black fur, and the others were a hodgepodge of black, brown, and white.

"There isn't a bad one in the lot," August stated, breaking Rita's solitude.

"I was just thinking that myself," Rita responded. "I want very much to know them all at once, and yet I know there's plenty of time."

"It might be a good idea to start hitching them up to the four-wheeler. You could run them up and down the road like Mark does with the others," August suggested.

"All right, but I doubt I'll be any good at it. It's been so long since I've even hitched a team. I've probably forgotten all about it," Rita answered.

"Don't worry about it, Rita. You'll do just fine, and if you need anything, Mark and I will be here to help."

Rita nodded and braved the question she'd been wanting to ask. "Why Mark? For a partner, I mean. Where's he from and why did you pick him?"

"I met him at church the summer you left home. He seemed like a good man. He had a great love of animals and from the start all he ever talked about was raising a sled team. I offered to help him. We've been working together ever since," August replied.

"I didn't realize you'd had a partner that long."

"I haven't. I just made him a partner last fall. He's a good, Christian man, Rita. I hope you'll give him a chance. I believe he was an answer to my prayers and your mother's," August stated, even knowing

46

that Rita thought very little about the power of prayer.

"I didn't even know you were looking for a partner," Rita said, trying not to sound too disappointed that her father hadn't confided in her.

"I guess I just started showing my age. The mornings got to be such a chore that all I wanted to do was stay in bed. I gave serious thought to getting rid of the dogs altogether, but I kept hoping you'd come home and fulfill your dream. So I hung on," August replied and added, "I suppose after you're gone, I'll sell out to Mark and let him take it all."

Rita fought back a sadness that threatened to materialize into tears. If her father was getting rid of the dogs, he must feel that his life was coming to an end. The dogs were everything to him, and Rita knew that August wouldn't part with them otherwise.

"Look," August said, noting Rita's sudden quietness, "God will take care of me, just as He always has. You'd do well to remember that and give it a little thought for yourself. You know I don't like to preach at you, but things haven't changed. I still worry about you, and I worry about your soul."

Rita hurried to embrace her father. "Don't worry about me, Daddy. I'm strong and quite capable of taking care of myself. You do what you have to, but don't worry about me."

Rita couldn't bring herself to admonish him for his reminder that she was still walking outside of God's truth. She was informed more often than not, by her mother, that she was the only one of the Eriksson children not to have made a decision for the Lord. It seemed to hang on Beth like a grievous weight.

Maybe that was why Rita clung stubbornly to her own nature. She refused to allow herself to think on the matter any further. God was only a tiny part of her worries. Mark Williams was quite another matter.

Chapter 4

Rita couldn't believe how quickly the summer passed. Before she knew it, the first heavy frost was upon the land, leaving an icy signature on the once-green valleys. The air was noticeably colder, and every morning Rita saw subtle changes that pointed clearly to the inevitability of winter.

The idea of snow and ice excited Rita. There was a quickening in her step and an energy unleashed that she'd not known existed. Daily, she ran the dogs and watched each one with careful interest, trying as she did to remember the things Mark and her father had told her to look for.

"Some dogs are just along for the ride," August had said, and Rita could see that this was true by watching the tuglines that connected the dogs to the gangline. She weeded out three dogs from the twenty-two simply because they refused to pull their own weight.

Others seemed prone to problems, sporting everything from simple injuries to the inability to keep up. They were hard workers but just not cut out for long distances. Rita had no choice but to eliminate them.

Rita spent much of her time in Mark's company, listening while he told her things that could well make a difference out on the trail. She remembered her father's caution to always carry dry kindling for long runs, as well as extra food and boots.

Days were long and arduous, usually starting by five in the morning and not ending until nine and sometimes ten at night. There was always the necessity of seeing to the dogs. Feeding, grooming, doctoring, running — all of these activities took precedence over nearly everything else. Then there was the work with the race sleds, harnesses, and assorted items that Rita would need to take with her when she raced the Iditarod. The work seemed never-ending and, as the student, Rita was frequently overwhelmed.

As autumn moved toward winter, Rita found herself actually enjoying the work and the company. It worried her, because often she found herself concentrating too much on what Mark was doing, whether it had anything to do with her training or not.

It was on one particular Saturday when Rita learned that Mark wouldn't be joining them that she actually found herself asking her father why.

"Mark has to fill in for one of the patrolmen," August replied to his daughter's question. He had come to notice that Rita was far more accepting of Mark's participation in her training. Maybe Rita was changing.

"So then," Rita said with a smile, "it'll be just you and me today?"

"You, me, and your mother," August replied without a thought.

"But, Mom's not out here with us," Rita commented. Her mother had never been one to take a great deal of interest in the kennel.

"I'm sure she's got enough to keep her busy in the house," August said, untangling a long length of rope. "She always has run a tight ship. Even when she owned that roadhouse near Northway. Her boarders never lacked for anything. I can vouch for that."

"I'm sure that's true," Rita answered and

sought to change the subject. "When do you think we'll get our first snow?"

"I'm not sure," August said, glancing up at the gray sky. "It doesn't feel like it just yet, but soon. Probably in another couple of weeks."

"I can hardly wait," Rita said wistfully. She longed to run the dogs on snow again and get the feel of handling the team behind a basket.

"You're doing good work," August said, offering the praise Rita craved. "I just know you'll be more than ready when March gets here."

"Dad, do you think I should run any of the shorter races first?" Rita took the rope from her father and hung it on a nearby nail.

"Rules say you have to have written proof of at least one sanctioned race of two hundred miles or more," August replied.

"Which races should I participate in?" Rita asked.

"You could warm up with some of the shorter sprint races. As far as a race of some distance, Mark thinks the Copper Basin 300 is your best bet. It's run in January and it's close to home. The terrain will be similar to that which the dogs are already used to and yet offer them the feeling of competition and crowds," August answered thoughtfully.

Rita remained silent while considering her father's words.

"It would give you a good chance to get to know some of the other racers and dogs," August continued. "And you might even make a name for yourself before the Iditarod."

"That could be bad, though," Rita replied. "It could put a lot of pressure on me to perform. Say I did really well in one race or another, then I'd be expected to achieve an even better performance in the Iditarod."

"That is a possibility," August said. "But, it could also be a challenge, and I know how competitive you can be."

"You sound like that's a fault and not an asset," Rita said with a frown. "There's nothing wrong with healthy competition."

"Healthy competition, no," August agreed. "However, competition can often lead to dangerous rivalry. Many mistakes are made by the person who thinks nothing of the rules and only of the achievement."

Rita shrugged off her father's concerns as she always had done in the past. It was impossible for him to understand her sense of competition. After all, he'd been an only son with a single sister to round out the family. He knew nothing of being the youngest of ten. When you were the baby of a huge family you always found yourself striving to make a place for yourself, Rita reasoned. Her father simply misunderstood her need.

"You know," August began, "I may sound a little old-fashioned, but I'd like for you to make your own sled."

Rita shook her head adamantly. "I wouldn't be any good at that. You know I've never had the touch for creating things that you have."

"But it's the only way to get a real feel for your equipment. Once you've been a part of creating the sled, it truly becomes a part of you. When it starts to run rough, you know instinctively what's wrong. When a piece breaks, you know from having created it just what's required to repair it," August answered.

"I guess that makes sense," Rita admitted. "But I don't know anything about it. You'll have a great deal to teach me."

"You're a quick student," August said with a laugh. "I tell you what, Monday we'll get started with the details."

"August," Beth called from the back

door. "Gerald's on the telephone. He wants to talk to you."

"I'm coming," August answered and turned to Rita. "You keep on sorting out these ropes and harnesses." Rita nodded and watched as her father headed toward the house.

She felt a twinge of disappointment in having to share her father with her oldest brother. She scarcely knew Gerald, even though he settled in Tok. Gerald and Phillip were her mother's sons from her first marriage. Rita had heard many times the story of how her mother and father met.

Her mother was a war widow, having lost her Canadian husband in World War II. Beth Hogan was running a roadhouse and trying to raise her children all alone when August had appeared to work on the Alcan Highway. Gerald and Phillip had appealed to August's heart, as had their mother, and, in no time at all, they became a family.

After that, many children came to bless the home of August and Beth Eriksson, but Rita saw it more as a curse. She hated being the youngest and felt completely insignificant to her family.

Plopping down on the ground, Rita tried

to ignore the anger she felt. Many people presumed that because she was the baby of the family, she surely would have enjoyed the most attention. However, nothing could have been farther from the truth.

"I've scarcely seen you," Beth commented, causing Rita to jump.

"I've been busy," Rita offered, refusing to look her mother in the eye.

"Yes, your father has told me," Beth replied. "He also tells me that you still seem very unhappy."

Rita's dark eyes flashed a warning as her head snapped up to meet her mother's face. "I'm just busy," she stated firmly. "This is hard work, you know." Rita knew the words sounded sarcastic, but she didn't care.

"You needn't take that tone with me, Rita," Beth said, standing her ground. "I won't cower beneath your anger and you can't wile your way around the issues with me. That's why you avoid me."

"I don't avoid you," Rita answered, tossing the harness aside and getting to her feet. "I avoid your preaching. You can't have a regular conversation with me. You never just want to know how I am or what I've been doing. You just want to pass judgment on me because I ruined your track record at church!"

Beth was noticeably hurt by the harsh words Rita hurled. "I'm sorry you feel that way, Rita. I do care about the things you're doing. I care very much."

"Yes, yes, I know. You care only because no matter what I do, it'll be wrong in your eyes," Rita said, trying to show nothing but the anger she felt inside. "I can't live up to your standards, Mother, so why not just give up?"

"I can't give up," Beth replied and pulled her sweater closer to ward off the cold. "It isn't my standards I want you to live up to. God's standards are the only ones that count."

"Yes, and you and God are like this," Rita said and intertwined her first two fingers.

"Don't take that tone with me," Beth snapped. Her anger was piqued — a typical reaction whenever she spoke with her youngest daughter about God. Why, out of ten children, was this one the most difficult? "I cherish my relationship with God," Beth continued. "He is the only constant in our lives. He is the only one that can offer us hope and eternal salvation. I only want you to come to understand His love for you."

"I've heard it all before, Mom," Rita answered impatiently. "I don't need your religion. I grew up all my life listening to preaching — yours, the pastor's, even Dad's. I've had enough preaching to last me a lifetime. Why can't you understand that I don't need a crutch like you do? I make my own way, and when I know what I want . . . I go after it."

"And what do you want, Rita?" Beth asked her daughter honestly.

"I want to live my life without restraints. I want to experience everything and anything. I don't want to be hemmed in by a list of do's and don'ts. Besides," Rita continued, "I don't see where your relationship with God has helped you in your relationship with me."

Beth swallowed hard to keep from snapping a retort. It was true. She struggled to have a decent relationship with her youngest daughter. There was always so much hostility to get through that Beth usually gave up long before Rita wore down.

"You are absolutely right. Our relationship lacks for much," Beth answered softly. "But, I'm always hopeful. You may have grown up and left home, but I will continue to endeavor to help you see the truth and God's love for you."

"It's always God's love, isn't it?" Rita questioned. "Never your love or our relationship. You use God like a shelter you can hide in whenever things get too tough. Learn to deal with me, one on one, Mom. I don't need this constant triangle. Then again," Rita said, turning to leave, "don't bother to deal with me at all."

Beth stood fixed to her spot as Rita walked off toward the creek. She was no longer shocked by her daughter's attitude and words. After all the years she'd sought to find a way to reach Rita, Beth had nearly given up trying. How could one child hold so much anger and hate inside and never give a clue as to where it came from or how it could be dealt with?

Walking slowly back to the house, Beth found herself whispering a prayer for Rita. It was really her only recourse, Beth decided. Rita had made it quite clear that she didn't want to talk about it, so Beth would leave her to God.

"Where's Rita?" August asked as he met Beth at the door.

"We had words," Beth admitted. "She stormed off to the creek and I'm here licking my wounds."

August enfolded Beth in his arms. "Don't lose hope, Bethany," he encouraged. "God has had worse cases to deal with."

Beth smiled. "She takes after her father where stubbornness is concerned."

"Ah, so you do remember," August replied with a grin. It had been Beth's honest determination that had led him back to God so many years earlier. "I guess I was just about as tough a nut as God ever had to crack. I remember feeling so angry that I couldn't join the army and fight in World War II. I blamed God for my misfortune of having no wife and no children. Now, I have ten beautiful children and a gorgeous wife, but only after I came back to Him first. Rita will come to understand the truth one day. We just have to hold on to that."

"I know you're right, August. But it hurts so much. Why does she hate me the way she does?" Beth questioned in a trembling voice.

"I don't believe she hates you, sweetie. I think she's just so miserable in herself and you are the closest reminder of what she could be if she turned her life over to God. I think that causes her more grief than she can own up to," August stated, giving Beth a squeeze. "You just keep praying, Mrs. Eriksson. Even the prodigal son in the Bible came home."

Beth tried to smile, but her heart was much too heavy. "Will you talk to her?" she questioned.

"For what it's worth," August said, dropping his hold on Beth. Beth nodded and watched for several minutes as August made his way past the pile of harnesses and ropes that Rita had left in disarray. She whispered a prayer for her husband and then another one for her daughter. Surely God could work a miracle in the heart of her hurting child.

"I thought I might find you here." August came upon Rita where she stood beside the icy creek. "I understand you and your mother had a fight."

"What else do we ever have? Certainly not a relationship." Rita's sarcasm hung thickly in the air.

August kicked at the dirt thoughtfully. "Your mother cares a great deal about you, Rita."

"Oh, I can certainly see that," Rita said sardonically and turned her back to her father. No sense in letting him see the tears that had formed in her eyes.

"I felt just like you did when I was younger," August remembered. "When I met your mom, I was a hard man with a grudge against God. I felt like God had disappointed me one time too many and therefore I didn't want anything more to do with Him."

"I've heard this story before," Rita muttered.

"I know," the aging August answered. "But, it seemed important to share it with you one more time. Your mom confronted me with my hard heart and, even though she loved me, she watched me walk away because she had the guts to stand up to me."

Rita said nothing. She stuffed her hands deep into her jeans pockets to ward off the chill. If only there was someplace to warm her frozen heart.

"Well, anyway," August said, running a hand through his salt-and-pepper hair, "I kept thinking about the things she'd shared with me and the way she assured me God was still there for me. I ran as far and as fast as I could and finally God pinned me down in a place I couldn't fight Him anymore."

"I know," Rita replied. "He buried you under a construction tractor after you fell over the embankment." Rita remembered the story from its many tellings. Her father's tractor had plummeted over a soft shoulder as he graded the roadway. He had been pinned beneath the equipment, broken and bleeding, and God had spoken to his spirit.

"I know it sounds silly," August admitted with a grin. "But sometimes God has to get your attention. He'd done everything else He could, but my stubbornness required drastic measures."

"Look, Dad," Rita began, turning to face her father. "Couldn't we just drop the subject? Isn't it enough that I know how you feel and you know how I feel?"

"You mean agree to disagree?" August questioned.

"Yes." Rita came to her father and put both hands on his shoulders. "I love you, Dad, and I need for you not to harp at me. Mother has preaching down to a fine art form, and I'd just as soon not have you hassling me as well."

"All right, Rita." August embraced his daughter. "I'll leave it be. At least for now."

"Thanks, Dad," Rita whispered. She couldn't help but wonder how she'd deal with her mother, but maybe if she put it off long enough, she wouldn't have to do anything about it. Maybe Beth would just leave well enough alone and realize that Rita was a grown woman with a mind of her own.

Chapter 5

The first snows fell and autumn quickly became winter. Rita was in better physical shape than she'd ever been, and her heart was eager for the challenge of the Iditarod.

After spending six months working with her dogs, Rita had chosen a team of fourteen, twice as many as the minimum requirement for the race. They were a hearty, well-bred group of dogs, and Rita felt a genuine pride whenever she worked with them.

Week after week, Rita found herself engulfed in conversations that dealt with the business of dogsled racing, conversations that made her eager to feel the icy winds upon her face and the solitude of the long trail.

"You have to remember," Mark told Rita as she worked to attach the brush bow to the front of her handmade sled, "it's not always best to be out in front. If you head out early in the race and find the trail blown over, you may break trail through hip-high snow . . . maybe even higher. That's tedious, exhausting work, and the dogs pay a toll for it as well as the musher."

"So it's better to pace yourself behind?" Rita questioned. She sat up and adjusted the hood of her insulated sweatshirt.

"Sometimes, but not always. It's a matter of attitude and decision. You have to keep your mind cleared of other clutter and totally devoted to the trail. Then the choices are easier to make. You have to have a feel for the course. When you're out there all alone and faced with decisions like where to make your camp and whether your dogs are up to another twenty miles without a rest, you realize that this is where experience, training, and attitude all make the difference between life and death."

"But how do you decide when it's right to take the risks when you've never run the Iditarod before?" Rita asked.

"Every Iditarod is different. No matter how many times you run it, you can't predict what the elements will be or how the terrain will have changed. Then, too, the route changes from year to year. From Anchorage to Ophir, it's the same trail for all years. After that, however, the northern route, during the even years, goes up to Ruby from Ophir and down the Yukon River to Nulato and Kaltag, to name a few. The odd year, the southern route leaves Ophir and goes down to Iditarod and across to Anvk. From there you follow the Yukon up to Kaltag, and then the race resumes identical trails again. And while I'm the first one to say that repeated experience on the trail is an important issue, it isn't everything."

Rita listened intently while Mark shared his secrets. She was still uncomfortable in his company, but she didn't feel the anger she once had. With so much else to concentrate on, Rita had less and less time to consider her lifelong struggle to find her niche.

"How's it going?" August asked as he joined Rita and Mark.

Rita gave her father a smile. "It's going slow," she replied honestly. "I told you this sled building thing wasn't my forte."

"But you've done very well," August encouraged. "Your first sled turned out great, and this lightweight racer will be even better. I think you're going to be pleased with the results."

"I think so, too," Mark agreed.

"I hope so," Rita said, thoughtfully checking her work for any errors.

"Are you two still planning on going out tomorrow?" August questioned, referring to the week-long sledding and camping trip that Rita and Mark had arranged.

"Yep," Mark answered before Rita could comment. "We're all set and the dogs are more than anxious. I figure we'll set out around dawn and be back in a week, maybe ten days."

"Just like we used to do when we were younger, eh, Rita?" August teased.

"Something like that," Rita replied. She was still uncertain about spending time away from her father and out on the desolate trail with Mark.

"Look, I'm going to finish up here and go home. I still have some gear to take care of and dog food to pack. I'll come over in the morning, and you be ready to leave by sunrise," Mark said, getting to his feet. "I hate being kept waiting," he added in a joking voice.

"Don't worry about me," Rita glanced upward. Her heart did a jump as she noticed Mark's warm brown eyes. She tried to steady her nerves and sound more severe than she felt. "I told you I could take care of myself," she added.

Mark laughed and gave a little bow. "Then I shall await the pleasure of your company on the trail tomorrow, ma'am." With that he was gone, and Rita stared after him, shaking her head.

"He's a good man, Rita," August said as if reading the question on his daughter's mind. "I trust him, and I know he'll take good care of you on the trail. Trust him, Rita. He might very well teach you something you don't know."

Rita nodded slowly and gave her father a brief smile. Trust him? She didn't even know him outside the realm of the Eriksson dog kennel. Why should she believe him to be so trustworthy?

"Dad?" Rita questioned with a sudden thought. "I'd like to have a pistol. May I borrow one of yours?"

August nodded. "That's a good idea. I'll make sure you have one for the Iditarod, too. Sometimes it's necessary to put down an animal. You can never tell when a moose is going to jump in the middle of your dog team. It's happened before, and they almost always have to be shot."

"I remember a moose wreaking havoc with one of the teams several years back," Rita agreed.

"I do, too," August replied. "I'll make sure you have what you need."

"I have you, Daddy." Rita jumped up to hug her father. "And you are all I'll ever need."

August embraced his daughter but said nothing. He certainly couldn't tell her what was in his heart. He couldn't explain that she needed the Savior and that without Him she would be hopelessly lost. Breathing a silent prayer, August gave his youngest daughter over to God, knowing that there was really little else he could do.

The wind had picked up and the sky threatened snow, but nevertheless, Rita and Mark, with lamps secured on their heads, mushed out into the darkness with their dog teams. They had decided to explore the area to the south and maybe even check out the trail for the Copper Basin 300.

The snow wasn't all that deep, but it had glazed over with ice from a recent warming and refreezing. It made a good trail, and Rita was surprised to learn that Mark had already spent many hours in the area, choosing the path they would take.

When they stopped for lunch, several hours later, Mark explained.

"I wanted this first day to be rather simple. You know, that way you could get used to the trail and being out away from civilization. And, it wouldn't be all that taxing for the dogs. We'll make camp about twelve miles down the way. There's a nice place by the river where we can set up camp under the trees. We'll have all the water we need and plenty of shelter," Mark told Rita.

"I didn't realize you had this all mapped out," Rita replied. She enjoyed some warmed-up tuna casserole her mother had sent along.

Mark stirred up the fire, enjoying himself and the freedom of the vast wilderness before him. "I am the teacher, remember?" His words were spoken in a gentle reminder, and for once Rita knew, in order to object, she'd have to work hard to conjure up her anger.

"I just meant that I didn't realize you'd spent so much time and preparation on this trip. I figured we were just kind of heading out into the great unknown," Rita answered.

"After today," Mark replied, "we will be. I haven't planned every detail out. Rest assured there will be many elements of surprise on our adventure." He lost himself for a moment looking into Rita's eyes. She quickly captured his heart. Turning away before Rita could perceive his thoughts, Mark called over his shoulder, "You ready to press on?"

"More than ready," Rita responded, unaware of Mark's emotions.

They broke camp and pressed to the south. The valley floor soon gave way to foothills and dense forests of black and white spruce, as well as aspen and birch. From time to time, stunted black spruce and the absence of hardwood trees betrayed the sure signs of permafrost ground. This was ground that never thawed, and nothing rooted well in its frozen subsoil.

It reminded Rita of the parable of the sower. The seeds that fell upon the rocky soil couldn't take deep root. She shook off the image, wondering why she'd even thought of it. No doubt eighteen years of Bible stories and Sunday school had to exist in memory somewhere. Sending the reminder of her mother and father's faith deeper within the dark recesses of her memories, Rita pressed on to keep pace with Mark.

Without warning, a snowshoe hare darted out across the trail, causing Rita's team to take off in a free-for-all chase. Rita struggled to keep her grip on the sled's handlebars. She wouldn't forgive herself if she lost her team, especially in front of Mark.

"Gee, Dandy!" she yelled above the barking huskies, trying to tell her dogs to go back around to the right. By now, they were nearly heading in the opposite direction from which Rita and Mark had been making their way. "Come gee! Dandy, come gee!" Rita called out. When Dandy finally heard his mistress's instructions, he managed to direct the team back to the trail, much to the disappointment of the other ten dogs behind him.

Rita tried not to look flustered, but she was keenly aware that Mark watched and evaluated her every move from where he'd brought his own dogs to a stop back on the trail. Expecting some sarcastic comment regarding the incident, Rita was surprised when Mark turned back around and called out the command that sent his dogs forward. Breathing a sigh of relief, Rita tried to be more prepared for any more interferences with her team.

Shortly before the last bits of muted sunlight faded from the sky, Mark brought them, without further mishap, to the place he'd planned for their first night on the trail.

Rita put up her small domed tent only after seeing to the needs of her dogs. August had explained to her on many occasions that the dogs were her life's blood on the trail. Taking care of them first insured that they'd be in prime condition to take care of her later.

Rita found spruce boughs and made beds for each of her dogs, while a roaring fire heated up August's personal choice of dog food. It was a hearty combination of commercial dog food blended with beef liver, vegetable oil, and eggs. All were chosen to give the highest degree of benefit to the active sled dogs.

With the dogs now fed and sleeping in fuzzy balls to ward off the minus-twenty-degree winds, Rita found herself able to settle down to preparing her own supper.

"I've already got the stew on the fire," Mark offered when he spied Rita digging into the food packs.

"I'm glad," Rita replied, plopping down beside the fire. "I'm absolutely starved." It felt good to sit and rest, even in frosty air that stung her eyes.

"I'd kind of like some coffee," Mark said,

pulling out a zippered bag of instant coffee.

"That does sound good," Rita agreed. While Mark found cups, Rita studied the surroundings. She realized how perfect their camp was. They were sheltered from the wind by a rocky ridge that followed the river for a short way. This was coupled with the canopy of spruce trees that lined the river.

They also had water — even if they did have to break the surface ice with an ax. With a little more effort, they soon had enough firewood to enjoy the evening, allowing both of them to sit back and bask in the warmth. Mark had been very wise to choose this place, Rita decided. A part of her wanted to tell him so; another part warned her not to make any kind of comment that betrayed her emotions.

Supper passed in relative silence. Mark seemed content to enjoy the quiet and the meal, while Rita nervously wondered how to relate to her traveling companion. Before their talk had always revolved around sledding, dogs, and the Iditarod. What if she were required to talk of something more?

As if reading her mind, Mark began to speak. "You know it's hard to sit out here in the middle of nowhere with all of this monumental beauty around you and not be in awe of it."

"It is impressive," Rita agreed in a guarded tone. "It makes it hard to consider leaving."

"Leaving?" Mark questioned. "Where would you go?"

Rita shrugged. "I don't know. I've thought about moving to Texas."

Mark chuckled. "Cowboys and oil wells instead of dogsleds and snow?"

"I don't know. It was just a thought," Rita replied. "I've always liked the things I've read about it. Lots of sunshine and wide open spaces. You can have it rustic and rural or live it up in the glamorous city night life. I guess Texas has a little bit of everything."

"Maybe I could call you 'Texas Rita,' " Mark joked, but Rita just lifted her chin defiantly.

"Maybe you wouldn't need to call me anything."

Mark hid his smile and turned away from Rita. There was no sense in irritating her further. "Look," Mark said and pointed to a glowing green light that loomed up from the horizon and grew in size until it seemed to fill the sky.

Rita watched as it changed in shape and size. The green soon gave way to a more prominent outline of pink and then, as the color intensified and darkened to a reddish hue, yellow fiery flickers sent fingers upward through the image to paint the sky.

"The northern lights," Rita commented as she watched the night show. "I've always loved them."

"I just don't know how anyone could watch them and doubt the existence of God," Mark said in a low, husky whisper.

"What's God have to do with it?" Rita said rather flippantly. "It's a natural phenomenon. I read all about it and it has something to do with the sun."

Mark turned from the light show to study Rita a moment before replying. "I don't understand how you could have spent years in church and fellowship with other Christians and say such a shallow thing."

Rita instantly felt defensive. Obviously, Mark was yet another devout Christian. Why hadn't she considered that before? There wouldn't have been any way at all that her father would have taken on a less than fully devoted man of God as his partner. Oh, she knew her father had told her Mark was a good man and a Christian, but since Mark had never bothered to make it an issue with her, Rita had felt safe to let things lie undisturbed.

"Look," Rita said with only the slightest hint of irritation in her voice, "I've tried to look at things like my folks, and apparently you do. I've joined all the groups, read all the Bible handouts, prayed all the prayers, and held my head just so when the minister preached his sermons. I've spent a lifetime being preached at, prayed at, and talked at and, as shallow as it might seem to you, I just don't feel the same way you do."

"I think that's the most honesty you've given me since we met," Mark remarked in a way Rita hadn't expected. It so flabbergasted Rita that she said nothing as Mark continued. "I know how hard it is to feel like God is real. I went through a bad time of that myself. People kept saying, 'Well, if you just believed the way you should, you'd understand.' Then they'd all kind of stand around with this knowing look, all nodding at each other like I'd missed the joke. I hated it."

"Exactly," Rita said, totally amazed that Mark actually had put her feelings into words. "Or they give you that little shake of their head, where you can practically hear the 'Tsk, tsk' under their breath, and they talk about turning you over to God to be dealt with. Like you were a sack of potatoes that needed to be washed up for dinner."

Mark chuckled out loud, momentarily breaking the tension. "My favorite one was when they'd tell me that my faith wasn't strong enough. Just have faith, they'd say. Faith is the key. Faith is the answer. Faith is your foundation. And then they'd never tell me how it was I was supposed to get it, keep it, or understand it."

"I can't believe we're having this conversation," Rita said suddenly. "My parents would never understand. Especially my mother."

"You and your mom have a difficult relationship, don't you?" Mark spoke the words hesitantly. He worried that if he prodded Rita to reveal too much, too soon, she'd bolt and run like a frightened deer.

"That's the understatement of the century. Negotiating peace among warring nations would be a simpler project than dealing with our relationship," Rita retorted.

"I would imagine that makes it quite difficult for you." Mark's words pulled Rita out of her defensive mode for once in her life.

"That's really the first time anyone has ever mentioned that our relationship might be hard on me. Usually, there's all this sympathy for my mother," Rita stated with a sadness to her voice. "She has a prayer group . . . you know the type. It's made up of the local church women and they all pray for the issues of the day. My mother never hesitates to tell me that they've been praying for me for roughly the last twenty-some years. It's no wonder that people see things her way. She probably goes to the meetings and pours out her heart and cries her miseries of life with a difficult child. It drove me from home and now that I'm back, nothing has changed."

"And exactly what is it that hasn't changed?" Mark asked, throwing another log on the fire.

Rita grew quiet for a moment, and Mark thought for certain he'd pushed her too far. When she finally spoke, he realized he'd been holding his breath and exhaled rather loudly.

"My mother can't deal with me as a daughter. I'm nothing more to her than a challenge. A soul to win to God so that her tally sheet is complete when she stands before her King. She's never cared for me as a mother would a child, and I resent the only concern she bears for me is that which is on the behalf of another."

"And this is also why you resist a relationship with God?" Mark asked without thinking.

"I picked up the Bible as a young girl," Rita said, turning. Mark's expression was gentle. "I was thinking about giving my life over to Him. I really was. But I opened the Bible to Isaiah and a verse that put me off in a way that even now causes me grief."

"What was it?"

"It said something like, 'As a mother comforts her child, so God comforts His people.' I'd never known anything but pain and frustration from my mother. Certainly not comfort. And if God was as comforting as my mother, then that meant nothing to me. I slammed the Bible shut and sulked for weeks. I had never felt more betrayed." Rita got to her feet and walked a few steps from the fire before turning around briefly. Her eyes narrowed slightly, blinking back tears. "I'm sorry. I should never have told you these things."

Mark watched Rita walk to the river's edge. She just stood there for several minutes, looking out as if seeking peace for her soul. He allowed her the time to compose herself before he joined her.

"I'm glad you talked to me," he whispered at her back. "I think it helps friends to understand one another when they know each other's pain."

"Friends?" Rita questioned, whirling around to find herself only inches from Mark. "I thought you didn't want to be my friend."

Mark smiled through the shadowy light. Rita noted the change in his eyes. "I'd like to be much more," Mark said before pulling Rita into his arms and kissing her.

Rita was shocked into silence and passive acceptance. She found herself enjoying the kiss, while she fought in her mind to resist the pleasure of Mark's touch. Warnings went off in her brain. Don't get too close! Don't care too much! Don't reciprocate!

When Mark released her, Rita shook her head and took a step backward. Mark reached out to steady her as she found her foot give way on the unstable riverbank.

"Let me go," she whispered without malice. She sidestepped Mark and felt his grip give way when her feet were fixed on firm ground. Without looking behind her, Rita hurried breathlessly to her tent and the solitude it afforded her.

Chapter 6

Rita returned from her sled trip more with-drawn and quiet than before. She purpose-fully went out of her way to avoid Mark, and very little was offered in the way of ex-planation.

August and Beth watched helplessly. How were they to help this child who so obviously didn't want their help? They sat alone in their kitchen one evening, long after Rita had retired for the night. Holding each other's hands as they shared a prayer, August and Beth found comfort in the Lord and each other.

"I'm really afraid for her," Beth said after August ended the prayer. "She's so miserable and unhappy with her life. She wants to blame everyone else for her prob-lems. Do you know that she told me she would never have bothered to come home except for the fact that her college roommate had decided to move to the Lower Forty-eight. Never mind the Iditarod. It was as if she couldn't accept that she'd made the choice to come home all by herself."

"I'd hoped things would be different," August admitted, pouring himself another cup of coffee. When he offered to pour Beth a cup, she shook her head.

"Did Mark say anything about their trip?" Beth questioned curiously.

"He mentioned that he kissed her," August said with a half-smile. "But she made it clear that he was to keep his distance and, well, you know Mark. He's a good man and he put it behind him."

"Does she still plan to race?" Beth asked.

"As far as I know," August answered with a shrug of his shoulders. "But with Rita, who can ever be sure. It wouldn't surprise me at all if she came downstairs tomorrow with her bags in hand." Beth nodded and said nothing. What else could be said?

Rita didn't show up the following morning with bags in hand, nor was her disposition as sour as it had been upon her return. She had just answered her mother's inquiry about what she'd like for breakfast when a knock sounded at the front door.

"I wonder who that is?" August put down his newspaper.

"I'll get it, Dad," Rita offered and took off for the front room.

"Aunt Julie!" August heard his daughter squeal in excitement.

"Julie?" August said and exchanged a look of surprise with Beth. "Julie said nothing about visiting." He got to his feet and met his sister and daughter halfway.

"Jewels," he said, using her nickname, "why didn't you tell us you were coming?"

"Sam and I wanted to surprise you," the white-haired Julie replied. She hugged August through her bulky knee-length coat.

"Where is your husband?" August questioned. He and Sam had been best friends long before Sam had married Julie. It must have been a lifetime ago when they'd all lived in Nome. "It's been years since I've seen him."

"You know Sam," Julie answered. "He's out there getting our things."

"I'll give him a hand," Rita said, but Julie waved her off.

"Don't bother," Julie replied. "There's already a nice young man out there helping him."

"That would be Mark," August offered. "He's the partner I wrote you about."

"Seems like a great guy," Julie said as Beth came into the room. "Bethany, you look great. Eastern Alaska must not take the toll on a body that western Alaska does. You look a hundred years younger than I feel."

Beth laughed and reached out to embrace Julie. "It's just the traveling that makes you feel that way. I know you. After a good rest, you'll be down here teaching me some new recipe or sewing shortcut."

"I told her this was a vacation," Sam called from the doorway. "She'd better take it easy. After all, that is what the doctor told her to do."

"Are you sick, Jewels?" August asked in a serious tone.

"I had pneumonia," Julie admitted. "But I'm much better now."

"Well, you will take it easy while you're here," Beth said, ushering Julie down the hall. "I have the perfect room for you. Remember the way the girls used to have the greenhouse bedroom all fixed up? Well, I have taken the project back on."

The group followed Beth to the bedroom. On one wall were huge double doors that Beth opened to reveal a greenhouse filled with potted plants.

"It's beautiful!" Julie exclaimed. "Imagine all that green in the dead of winter."

"It's well insulated, too," August said, moving aside for Mark to bring in the luggage he'd wrangled away from Sam.

"By the way," Mark said and placed the bags on the highly polished, wooden floor, "I'm Mark Williams."

Sam took his hand and shook it vigorously. "You know who I am already, but this here is my wife, Julie. She's August's sister."

"Yes, I know," Mark replied as he took Julie's hand and held it. "August has spoken most fondly of you."

Julie exchanged a look of love with her brother. They had always been close, and even when August had moved so far from Nome, he'd managed to keep Julie and Sam as important parts of his life.

Rita took the opportunity to slip from the room. She hated herself for leaving without getting an opportunity to talk with her aunt, but there would be time for that later.

She quickly made her way to the back porch, where she retrieved her insulated coveralls and boots. She had finished dressing to tend the dogs, when Mark appeared.

"Are you going to keep avoiding me?" he asked in a gentle voice.

Rita made the mistake of meeting his eyes. "I, uh . . ." Her words trailed into silence. She wanted to say more, but the words were stuck in her throat.

"Well?" he pushed.

"I don't want to talk about it," Rita stated firmly and started past him.

"Rita," Mark called and took hold of her arm.

"I don't want to talk to you right now," Rita repeated. "Don't you understand? You are annoying me with this pressure."

"What are you afraid of?" Mark asked her. He dropped his hand and waited for her reply.

Rita's eyes flashed the warning that her anger had been piqued. "I'm not afraid of anything, and I don't owe you any explanations. You've trained me now, and I can make the Iditarod a reality without any more interference from you."

"Where is all this fury coming from?" Mark asked. "Is this because I kissed you or because you opened up to me?"

Rita quickly lowered her head to avoid Mark's reading her eyes. She knew that saying nothing was like surrendering, but in truth, she was afraid to say anything. Pushing past him, Rita made her way to the dogs.

Mark stood on the steps watching her walk away. When had he come to care so much about this hurting woman-child? He was almost afraid to search himself for the depth of his concern. What if he learned more than he was willing to deal with?

Rita's opportunity to speak in private with her aunt Julie presented itself the following morning. Beth and August had volunteered to take Sam and Julie shopping in Tok, and when Julie chose instead to stay home, Rita offered to keep her company.

Preparing them both some hot tea, Rita took two steaming mugs with her to Julie's greenhouse sitting room.

"I'm so glad you came here," Rita stated bluntly, handing Julie the tea. "I've always been able to talk to you, even when I couldn't talk to Mom or Dad. You never seemed to judge me or make me feel inadequate."

"I knew you needed me," Julie replied. "I felt the most overwhelming need to keep you in my prayers and not for the reasons you think, so stop frowning. I'm not going to start preaching at you, I just knew you needed some extra care."

"Thanks," Rita managed, a bit uncomfortably.

"Now, why don't you tell me what's bothering you?" Julie smiled.

For the next two hours, Rita shared her heart with her aunt. She mentioned her mother's attitude and her worries about her father's advanced years, at which Julie only laughed.

"We aren't that many years apart you know," Julie remarked. "And I feel fit as a fiddle. Of course, Sam and I know we aren't young kids anymore. In fact, it wouldn't surprise me at all if one of us were to die in the near future."

Rita frowned at her aunt's words. "I don't like to think about that. I don't know how you can talk so unemotionally about it, either."

"Rita, you don't like to talk about it because you're young and because you don't know what the future holds for you after death. That's all. Sam and I aren't afraid to die. Oh, we don't like the idea of the separation here on earth, but we know that it won't be for long, and then we can share eternity in heaven."

"You make it sound so wonderful,"

Rita replied with a weak smile. "I know that Dad feels the same way. I guess it's just my selfishness that keeps me worried."

"Rita, I think it's fear, not selfishness that keeps you bothered. For all of your life, I've never seen you a single time without fear in your eyes. What is it that you're so afraid of?"

The words rang in her ears. Mark had asked her the same question. What was she afraid of?

"I don't know," Rita answered with a heavy sigh. "I try not to believe that I'm afraid of anything. It makes you vulnerable to be afraid."

"And vulnerability is probably what you fear the most," Julie replied. "Vulnerability means that you aren't one-hundred percent in control. Vulnerability means that someone might see something more than the façade of independence you wear. Vulnerability might mean that someone will get too close to you."

"Yes," Rita admitted.

"Why do you fear getting close to others?" Julie asked softly.

Rita put her cup down and paced the room. "I don't know. I guess because it hurts so much when they reject you."

"And who rejected you, Rita?" Julie pressed on.

"Lots of people," Rita answered. "My brothers and sisters never had much to do with me. Even my own mother . . ." Her thoughts fell short of words. "I don't really want to talk about them. I'm having a problem, however, with Mark Williams."

"He seems nice enough," Julie replied.

"He is," Rita said and stopped. "That's the problem. I've managed to put off every guy who's ever shown the slightest bit of interest in me. I knew I wanted to go to college and become a nurse like you, and I knew that someday I wanted to race in the Iditarod. A man would interfere with that."

"I once worried about the same thing," Julie laughed. "It's so like God to put you through something so that you can be a help to someone else later down the road."

"What are you talking about?" Rita questioned.

"When I married Sam, I did so without ever really understanding how he felt about my career as a nurse. Remember, my job was with the Public Health Department and I was often dogsledding out to the villages for many weeks at a time. I didn't know how to talk about my fears to

Sam. I just knew that he would never approve."

"But he did, didn't he?"

"Yes, he did," Julie remembered. "He had it all planned out ahead of time to be with me on the trail. So for the most part, Sam joined me whenever I had to be gone for long periods of time. Eventually, I learned we were to have a baby, and so I quit my job and planned to stay home for a spell. Of course, you know that our son died when he was very small."

Rita nodded. "Why didn't you have other children?"

"I wanted to. I learned that I was to have another baby only three months after little Sam's death. But, I miscarried and nearly bled to death. They had to perform a hysterectomy and that meant no more children."

"I'm sorry, Aunt Julie," Rita said sadly. "I never knew."

"It's all right, Rita. God had other plans for Sam and me. We learned a great deal just being together, and we worked well as a team among the Eskimos and Indians. I have no regrets and have thoroughly enjoyed my life. But in order to do so, I became very vulnerable."

"I can well imagine," Rita said in a

barely audible voice. "I'm just not sure that I could deal with it as well."

"A body never knows what it can endure until it goes through it. You're planning on putting yourself to a test of the elements when you race from Anchorage to Nome. You will be vulnerable because of the position you place yourself in. Do you want to back away from the responsibility of the Iditarod just because of that challenge?" Julie asked her niece.

"Well, no," Rita shook her head.

"You like this Mark, don't you?" Julie questioned again. "That's why this situation has become so disturbing to you. It's why your mother's words about God are so frightening to you. You know the truth about God. How could you not? You were raised in an atmosphere of Christian love. You attended church on your first outing after birth. Yet, even with all of this knowledge and wisdom at your fingertips, you chose instead to turn away from God's love. Why is that, Rita?"

"I don't know," Rita answered, forgetting to be angry that Julie had referenced salvation.

"I think you do," Julie replied. "You don't trust yourself enough to love God or Mark."

"What?" Rita questioned as her head snapped up to meet her aunt's eyes. "What in the world has trusting myself got to do with loving God or Mark?"

Julie shifted uncomfortably in the wicker chair. Rita jumped up to retrieve a pillow while she waited for her aunt's insight.

"Thank you, dear," Julie said as she eased against the cushioning bulk. "Now, what I was trying to help you see is the huge mistrust you have in yourself. I think you're the only one who can say why it's there, but its effects are clear. God stands with open arms, offering a free gift of love and salvation. Mark apparently offers at least friendship, possibly more. In both cases, I don't believe it's God or Mark who frightens you the most. It's Rita. For whatever reason you have contrived, you don't believe yourself trustworthy and deserving of love."

Rita frowned and bit at her lower lip. Was her aunt Julie right? Was this the demon from which she had so long run? Sitting back down, Rita seemed to withdraw into her thoughts to find the answers.

Julie reached out and covered Rita's hand with her own. "I know this is hard for you, but may I suggest something?"

Rita nodded.

"Good. I want to outline some Scripture for you. Maybe you can better understand what I'm saying and what God's plan is, if you read His Word. Now, don't get defensive with me, just trust me. I want you to read the verses I mark and just think about them. Then, if you want to talk to me about them, I'll be happy to share whatever I know. Deal?"

Rita hesitated for a moment. She looked into Julie's dark eyes. Eyes that held so much love and concern for Rita that she wanted to cry for the very need of it.

"All right, Aunt Julie," she finally answered. "It's a deal."

"And Rita," Julie added with a smile, "try not to be so hard on that young man. I think your father is an excellent judge of character. After all, he led me to my Sam. Mark may very well be a special gift for you. Maybe he'll only be a friend, maybe more. But you'll never know if you aren't decent to him. Just open your heart a bit. You might be surprised at the results."

Rita nodded slowly. "I'll try. But it's those results that I'm worried about."

Chapter 7

Rita sat in the quiet solitude of her room. For the first time since she'd stopped going to church, she found a Bible spread out before her. Her aunt Julie had given her several Scriptures to look up, and most of them were in the first book of Corinthians.

Rita knew the Bible forward and backward, and as she turned to the thirteenth chapter of Corinthians, she already knew what the verses would say.

"If I speak in the tongues of men and of angels, but have not love, I am only a resounding gong or a clanging cymbal," the first verse began. Rita scanned the verses, remembering them well. She once had to quote the verses from memory in order to win a new Bible. It hadn't meant that much to her, but it seemed terribly important to her mother and father.

Then Rita quoted the fourth, fifth, and

sixth verses aloud. "Love is patient, love is kind. It does not envy, it does not boast, it is not proud. It is not rude, it is not self-seeking, it is not easily angered, it keeps no record of wrongs. Love does not delight in evil but rejoices with the truth."

Rita stopped and thought immediately of her mother. *Love keeps no record of wrongs,* she thought. So much had passed between them. So many angry words, so much ugliness and hurt. If love truly kept no record of wrongs, then maybe Rita didn't love her mother.

It was as though she'd had the wind knocked out of her. Rita had realized the anger and distance she felt toward her mother, but never once had she considered that she might not love her.

Glancing down at the Bible, Rita read on about how love does not delight in evil but rejoices with the truth and that it always protects, always trusts, always hopes, always perseveres. She didn't feel that way at all toward her mother. She didn't trust her mother or understand her. How could she love her?

The realization bothered Rita more than she could bear. Where had they gone wrong? From where had the pain come? Rita stretched out across her bed and closed her eyes. In her mind she saw herself as a child, long black pigtails trailing down her back. Her mother had always insisted that Rita wear her hair long and Rita, in turn, hated it. But why?

Rita saw herself playing alone in her room. There were no other siblings her own age and nobody seemed to notice that she was lonely.

"Go play, Rita," she could hear her mother saying. She was fitting one of Rita's older sisters for her wedding dress.

"There's nobody to play with," answered a five-year-old Rita.

"Then just find something to do, Rita. I'm busy!" her mother had exclaimed in complete frustration.

Rita had walked away from the room, head hanging down like one of the dogs after being told "no" to some forbidden activity. She had almost made it to her room before hearing her mother tell her sibling how hard it was to live with Rita. There were other words, too. It was more pain than Rita wanted to deal with. Opening her eyes she thought instead of Mark Williams.

She couldn't deny that she enjoyed his kiss. Nor could she ignore the way her heart had jumped at his touch. She saw his face in her mind and the soft, gentleness of his eyes. Rita buried her face in her pillow. Why were these things happening just when she should be clearheaded and single-minded. The race was in such a short time, and Rita knew she needed to devote her thoughts to it.

"If I hadn't read the Bible," Rita thought aloud, "this wouldn't be happening. This is why I don't like all this soul searching. It brings up things I'd rather not think of."

Rita thought of her aunt Julie's words about trust. Rita didn't trust people and she didn't trust herself. Trusting meant opening yourself up to more hurt. It meant being vulnerable, and Rita believed when a person was vulnerable, others took advantage of you.

Rita was just starting to doze off when a knock sounded at the door. Getting wearily to her feet, Rita opened the door to find her father.

"Am I interrupting anything?" August asked.

"No, come on in, Dad. I was just about to go to bed." Rita stepped back.

August walked into the room and pulled Rita's desk chair up beside her bed. He noticed the Bible and although he wanted to ask about it, August decided to let Rita bring it up.

"It's kind of early for you to be going to bed, isn't it?" August questioned. "You aren't sick, are you?"

"No, Daddy," Rita said with a smile. "I'm just tired. It's been an exhausting day with the dogs, and then, of course, I've been doing a great deal of thinking about the race and all the complications and problems we still have to overcome."

"There is a lot to consider," August agreed. "We need to finish buying your supplies for one thing. Then we have to arrange for transporting dog food and whatever else you'll need to the various checkpoints on the trail. I thought I'd send you and Mark over to Fairbanks tomorrow."

"Fairbanks? But that'll take a whole day coming and going," Rita protested. "Can't we get everything we need in Tok?" What she really wanted to say was that she couldn't imagine having to bear Mark's company for a whole day without revealing her feelings. Then again, what were her feelings?

"We'll get some of the stuff in Tok, but there are several things I want you to pick up in Fairbanks," August replied.

"I could go alone," Rita offered.

"No," August answered. "Mark has things to pick up, as well. You'll need his help, and I know he'll enjoy your company."

"Why do you say that?" Rita asked, suddenly interested in what Mark might have said to her father.

August grinned. "It isn't hard to see that he cares for you."

"Has he said that?"

"Well, I suppose it wouldn't be fair to share our conversations with you. But, suffice it to say, his opinion of you is quite high." August reached out to take Rita's hand. "I get the feeling you're kind of fond of him as well."

Rita couldn't contain her surprise. "I don't know what you're talking about."

"Rita, this is me you're talking to," August said softly. "I've seen the way you watch Mark, and I've seen the way he watches you. I know there's a chemistry there, but I also know there are a lot of problems to overcome. Please believe me, I'm not trying to push a romance between you two. I just realize that you share an interest. Mark's a good man, Rita. You could do a lot worse."

"I know," Rita said, finally giving in. "He is nice, and I do enjoy his company. I'm just not ready for any relationships. I hope you understand. I mean, I know you worry about me being alone, but don't. I'll be fine, Daddy."

"I don't think you're as tough as you'd like any of us to believe, Rita. But, nonetheless, I'll bide my time," August stated. "Now, are you up to the trip tomorrow?"

"Sure, but I really need to be careful. I'm running out of money fast," Rita answered.

"I've sold a couple of dogs," August said. "We have to have enough set aside to ship the supplies to the checkpoints, as well as the one thousand two hundred forty-nine dollars that it takes to register in the Iditarod. Your mother is making your dog booties and some of your insulated gear."

"She is?" Rita questioned in amazement.

"That's right. She's also freezing snacks for your dogs. She's making honeyballs right now," August said, referring to a popular treat that many sledders used. The treats were made of lean beef, honey, powdered eggs, brewer's yeast, and vegetable oil. To this, vitamins and bonemeal were added and rolled into pieces the size of baseballs. It gave the dogs a tasty, high-protein snack that helped to meet the 10,000 calories a day that each dog needed to sustain energy on the trail.

Rita said nothing. She'd had no idea her mother was involved in making her Iditarod dream come true. It made Rita uncomfortable. Somehow it made her feel vulnerable.

"Now, have you kept track of the mandatory requirements?" August continued. "You know about the maximum ratings on the sleeping bag and the minimum weight requirements?"

"Sure, Daddy," Rita said, and recited the requirements for both. "I also need an ax with a head weighing at least one and three-quarters pounds, and the handle has to be at least twenty-two inches long. Then I need a pair of snowshoes thirty-three inches by eight inches, eight booties for each dog, one cooker, one pot capable of holding three gallons of water, two pounds of food for each dog, and one day's rations for myself. Oh, and it all has to fit on the sled. Did I leave out anything?"

August laughed. "Not as far as the mandatories go. You've done your homework, and I'm very proud of you. When you and Mark get back from Fairbanks, we'll start going over the critical points of the route itself." August got to his feet and studied his youngest daughter for a moment. She was willowy and graceful, but there was still a hardness to her that he didn't understand. "I love you, Rita," he said, turning to leave.

"I love you, too, Daddy," Rita called out. She noted the look of concern on her father's face and hoped silently that he wasn't feeling ill. She couldn't help but notice the way he seemed to slow down more and more each day.

Long after their conversation, Rita still lay awake in bed thinking of her father's interminable aging. She wished she could have known him as a young man, wished he could have parented her as a young man. With thoughts interwoven with images of Mark Williams, Rita finally fell into a restless sleep. Tomorrow she would spend a great deal of time alone with Mark, and the thought weighed as heavy on her mind as that of her father's strength and health.

For most of the trip into Fairbanks, Rita allowed Mark to set the conversation. She answered only when the situation required her to do so and refrained from offering her opinion when it did not. She stared out the window watching the endless spruce forest, now heavy with snow. The trees seemed to weave an impenetrable labyrinth across the landscape and Rita wished silently that she could lose herself out amongst them rather than travel in confinement with Mark.

Mark sensed Rita's reluctance to open up to him even before they'd climbed into his truck for the long trip. He wondered if her silence was due to her efforts to concentrate on the upcoming race or something more personal.

Their business in Fairbanks passed swiftly and satisfactorily, and Rita was grateful that Mark had to see to many of his own needs. Before Rita slipped away to take care of a personal matter for her father, they agreed to meet back at the truck by three o'clock.

The jeweler's shop for which August had written the address was only a block away from where Rita had parted company with Mark. She walked into the building, jingling the bells on the front door as she did. A gray-haired man in a dark blue business suit met her before she reached the counter.

"May I help you?" he asked in a rich baritone voice.

"I'm here to see Mr. Simons," Rita related. "My father sent me with this package and instructions that I am to pick up a gift he ordered for my mother."

"You must be Rita Eriksson," the man replied. "I'm Jim Simons." He extended a friendly hand forward that Rita took with less enthusiasm.

"I'm glad to meet you. This is the package my father sent me with," Rita stated, quickly dropping the man's hand. She handed the heavy box to Mr. Simons, halfway expecting him to open it. When he didn't, Rita couldn't contain her surprise. "If you need to look it over," she said, "I have time to wait."

"That isn't necessary at all," Mr. Simons replied. "Your father and I have already arranged the matter. I have your mother's gift already wrapped." Mr. Simons moved to the back side of the counter, where he placed the package Rita had brought and retrieved a smaller, gift-wrapped box. "He'll find everything in order."

Rita nodded and took the gift.

"May I show you anything?" the man questioned. "I have some lovely necklaces just in and also there's a sale on some of my finest rings."

"I don't think so, thank you," Rita said with a glance at her watch. "I have to meet Mark, I mean my ride, at three o'clock and

I still have a few more stops to make."

"Would your companion be Mark Williams?" Mr. Simons asked, surprising Rita.

"Why, yes," Rita answered. "How did you know?"

Mr. Simons laughed. "I guess that does seem a bit strange, doesn't it. I seemed to recall your father mentioning that you and Mr. Williams would be riding into town together. I have the wedding ring Mr. Williams picked out when he was here last weekend, and I presumed he would stop by today and pick it up. I wasn't certain, however, that it would be ready so I didn't call him ahead of time. If you would be so kind as to tell him that it's finished, I would sincerely appreciate it."

Rita felt as though she'd been delivered a blow. A wedding ring! Mark had never mentioned having a girlfriend, much less someone he planned to marry. Trying hard to keep her astonishment to herself, Rita agreed to pass Mr. Simons's message on to his client.

Walking from the store, Rita tried not to let the news bother her. Of course Mark was free to see whomever he chose and marry whenever he decided to, but Rita was amazed that her father hadn't even alluded to the fact that Mark was dating someone. In fact, Rita thought, her father had pushed her toward a relationship with Mark. Maybe he didn't know that Mark planned to marry someone else.

Unless . . . Surely Mark hadn't bought the ring for Rita! No, Mark wouldn't do things that way. He was too straightforward and honest. Honest to a fault, she thought.

Rita hadn't realized the apprehension and disappointment that was creeping into her heart. Had she really become more interested in her father's rugged business partner than she'd allowed herself to see?

"He's getting married," Rita muttered under her breath. "I would never have guessed it in a million years."

She made her other stops, barely able to concentrate on what she was doing, and made her way back to where Mark sat waiting in the pickup.

"Well, Texas Rita, get everything you were after?" he asked with a good-natured smile.

"I guess so," she answered, not even acknowledging the nickname. Rita looked up at him as if really seeing him for the first time. She felt saddened to realize they would never be more than friends. How could she have been so blind to the fact that she was falling in love with Mark Williams?

"Well then, we'd best head home. We can stop and pick up something to eat on the way out of town. That is, if you don't mind fast food," Mark said, reaching down to start the truck.

"I don't mind," Rita replied. She suddenly remembered Mr. Simons's request and reached out to prevent Mark from starting the engine. "I almost forgot. I had to pick up something for Dad at Simons's Jewelry Store. Mr. Simons said to tell you that your package is ready."

Rita watched purposefully to catch Mark's reaction. He smiled broadly and patted his coat pocket. "I've already taken care of it," he answered.

Rita thought he seemed quite pleased with himself. She fastened her seat belt and nodded. "Then I'm ready to go," she said and turned to stare out the passenger window.

Aside from giving Mark her order for a hamburger, french fries, and iced tea, Rita was silent in her brooding.

"How could I have been so stupid as to let my guard down and get interested in him?" she whispered to herself. She sighed and accepted the food that Mark had generously paid for.

Wasn't this exactly why she didn't allow herself to be vulnerable? The pain she was feeling brought it all back to her. She had to build the wall up higher to protect herself from ever feeling this way again. How could she have been so stupid?

Of course, she reasoned with herself, *I never gave Mark the slightest bit of encouragement. He had no reason to believe I was interested.* Rita made a pact with her heart that from that moment forward, she would care about nothing else but the Iditarod. She wouldn't allow herself to care about anyone else in a way that would distract her from accomplishing her dream of racing and completing the Iditarod.

From now on, Rita vowed silently, Mark was nothing more than the rival she'd originally seen him as and, despite her aunt Julie's encouragement to be less severe with him, she wouldn't allow him even an inch into her life.

Mark was baffled by Rita's silent treatment. Just when he thought she was thawing a bit and starting to open up to him — bang! She always slammed the door in his face.

When they got back to Rita's house,

Mark started to say something about it, but Rita darted quickly from the truck and nearly ran into the house. What was with her, anyway?

Mark started unloading the supplies, and August soon came out to join him. August immediately noticed the furrows that lined Mark's forehead and knew the cause was most likely Rita.

"You want to talk about it?" August asked, following Mark into the shed where they stored dog supplies.

"I suppose that would be the logical thing," Mark said, slamming a fifty-pound bag of commercial dog food to the ground. "However, I'm not feeling very logical. I'm confused and frustrated, but that's nothing unusual after spending the day with your daughter."

August grinned; he knew how infuriating Rita could be. "What happened?"

"I don't even know," Mark began. "She was reserved as always when we headed out, but by the time we got to Fairbanks, I thought she was starting to relax a bit. I figured on having a really nice trip home. You know, maybe talk through some of our feelings, but she was quieter than ever and never offered me so much as a single word."

August frowned and followed Mark to the truck. "She never said a word? She didn't even fight with you?"

"Nope," Mark replied and hoisted another bag of dog food on his shoulder.

"That's not like her," August said. "She must have it bad for you."

Mark nearly dropped the feed. "What? I just told you she wasn't even speaking to me. How can you say she has it bad for me?"

"Because Rita fights with people she doesn't care about. If the relationship isn't that important to her, she won't be put down, cast aside, or trod on in any manner. However, if she has feelings for you and the relationship is important to her, she handles it totally differently. Look at her and her mother. They scarcely share two words. Now, on occasion they will argue, but Rita hardly ever handles it in the same flippant manner she does when dealing with strangers," August stated. "Rita cares for you, Mark, of this I'm certain. Her silence speaks more clearly than any words could."

"Then what do I do?" Mark asked seriously.

"Pray for her, Mark. Pray good and hard for her. I found the Bible open on her bed the other night. I think the Lord is really working her over and she needs to come to terms with Him first."

Mark nodded. "I'll pray."

Inside the house, Rita found herself face-to-face with another mountain of emotion — her mother. Beth had purposefully sought out her daughter in order to take some measurements for Rita's insulated pants.

"Did you enjoy your time with Mark?" Beth asked innocently.

"Why?" Rita snapped, rather irritably. "Why do you ask that?"

"I just thought maybe you and he —"

"Well, don't think about him and me," Rita interrupted. "There is nothing to think about. He's my trainer along with Dad, nothing more."

"You sound awfully firm on the matter," Beth said, taking the final measurement.

"I am," Rita replied. "Getting close to people only hurts you when they don't return your feelings."

Chapter 8

"I can't believe you sold them!" Rita nearly yelled the words. "How could you give up your Iditarod ingots, just to finance me in this race?"

"They weren't that important to me," August said with a shrug. "And I didn't think they were that important to anyone else."

Rita stomped her snowy boots against the straw-covered floor of her father's supply shed. "Well, they were to me," she finally said. She tried to ignore the fact that Mark was sitting not three feet away.

"Look, Rita," August began, "Mr. Simons wanted to make them into tourist necklaces. He paid me more than I deserved to be paid because he's a fair man and knows that by adding a simple silver chain to each, he'll net a small fortune. Added to that I sold four more dogs. Now we have enough money to travel in style and keep everyone fed and healthy. Don't begrudge me doing things my way, Rita. It's important for me to see you accomplish this. It may be your only chance to ever compete. Don't spoil it now."

Rita bit back a retort and nodded her head. "If that's what you want, Dad," she murmured.

"Good," August said with a smile. "We've got a lot of work to do and a great deal of information to go over. Mark, did you bring your notes on the trail?"

"Yup." Mark got to his feet, patting the pocket of his insulated overalls. "They're right here."

"Well, why don't we get started then. Let's go into the office where it's warm," August suggested, and the other two followed his lead.

Mark set aside his gloves and pulled a thick packet of papers from his pocket. Rita and her father joined him at the small table. "It's important to keep checking your list of supplies. You never know when you'll leave something out," Mark began the conversation.

Rita nodded and tried to quell the rapid beat of her heart when Mark gave her a quick wink.

"You know the mandatory items, but you've got important decisions to make about the rest of your gear. Most mushers on the Iditarod don't bother with the weight of a tent, they usually sleep on the sled or at one of the offered shelters —"

"If they sleep," August interrupted. "I don't imagine I got more than seven hours that first week."

Mark nodded and added with a laugh, "I think that's why they insist on the mandatory layovers. There's the twenty-four-hour one that you must take at one time or another and a six-hour stop in White Mountain before the final push to Nome."

"Where do you take the twenty-four-hour stop?" Rita asked.

"A lot of folks take it at Rohn," answered Mark. "You've just come through the mountains, and you're physically and emotionally drained. There's good shelter, food, and water there, and the people are great, too, but we're getting a little ahead of ourselves. First, you have to get that far."

"I'll get there," Rita said in a determined way that left both men little doubt that she would.

"There are other things to consider," Mark continued. "We'll head down to Anchorage in plenty of time to have the race-appointed veterinarians check out the dogs. You have to have all the shots up to date for parvovirus, rabies, and distemper."

"I have the records for all of that," August assured them. "You'll be given the Official Iditarod Cachet to carry with you. This is promotional material from the racing committee. It usually weighs about five pounds and has envelopes to be post-marked in Anchorage as well as Nome. It kind of celebrates the fact that the Iditarod trail is the old mail trail. The top finisher's envelopes are usually auctioned off to raise money for the race."

"Sounds like I'll have a crowded sled basket," muttered Rita.

"That's why what you choose to take along is so critical," Mark said, meeting Rita's dark eyes. He wished silently that he could find some sign of closeness in them, but Rita was expert at masking her feelings, and he saw nothing. "You can always dump stuff off as you go, but you can't get what you need in the middle of the Alaskan interior when you realize you've neglected to bring something."

"That's true," August stated. "I ran low on headlamp batteries early on and then I forgot to pack an extra pair of boots as well. When I got my only pair soaking wet and the windchill made the temperature seventy below zero, I knew I'd just cashed in the race."

Rita nodded, remembering how her father always reminded her to take extra boots whenever she and Mark trekked out into the wilds.

"Boots, extra clothes, batteries, lightbulbs, gloves, ropes, harnesses, even sled runners are all things you'll have to choose carefully. You must also be able to transport any injured or ill dog on that sled and, in a pinch, sleep in it instead of on top of it. You have to be careful, and you have to be smart," Mark added.

Rita tried to absorb it all. She wanted very much to show both Mark and her father that she was fully capable of caring for herself. It was a dangerous position to put herself in, because with her prideful attitude, she purposefully avoided asking important questions, questions that could very well mean the difference between life and death.

"There are also rules of the road," Mark continued. "You'll get most of these on paper, but some are just givens. There's the Good Samaritan Rule that says no racer can be penalized for helping another in an emergency. You have to explain the incidents to the race official at the next checkpoint, but there shouldn't be any problems."

"Also, there are regulations related to the wildlife. If you have an incident arise where wildlife has attacked you, there are rules that relate to the situation. If the game is killed in defense of life or property, you are responsible to get that animal gutted and cared for," August remarked.

"But that could take a long time and by then you'd lose your place in the race," Rita said irritably. "That doesn't seem fair."

"No other racer can proceed ahead of you," Mark said, setting the record straight. "You don't lose your place." Was it Rita's imagination, or did Mark sound rather disgusted with her?

"If it's impossible to take care of the animal, for whatever reason," August continued, "you need to report the incident to the racing committee."

Rita nodded, still disturbed by Mark's intonation.

"Of course, we don't have to worry about cruelty to the animals," Mark began, "but rule number thirty of the Dog Procedures states that racers aren't allowed to commit any action or inaction that causes preventable pain or suffering."

"And they are quite severe on this rule," August added. "Violation of this rule results in disqualification. The whole world watches the Iditarod with extreme concern for the health and safety of the animals. It's almost as if it doesn't matter what happens to the drivers as long as the dogs are pampered and cared for. Now, don't get me wrong," August continued, "I believe the dogs should always be cared for first. It's what I've taught you since you first started working with them. Your dogs are your life's blood out there. You feed them first, bed them down first, go over their bodies for injuries or problems, all before you take any form of personal comfort."

"I know all of that, Dad," Rita articulated.

"We're just trying to help you remember," Mark joined in. "There's so much that you must keep in mind." Mark noted the frown on Rita's face. "Look, Rita, no one is trying to make you feel stupid. We know that much of what you need to be aware of will come second nature to you. But, there will be those things that don't, and they'll probably be the very things that will not only make or break the race for you, but may result in a great many problems for you if you aren't on top of them."

"Okay. Okay," Rita retorted. "I'm all ears."

"Well, let's get on with the race itself," August suggested.

"That sounds good," Mark agreed. "Now first of all is Anchorage to Eagle River. This is mostly urban and, as much as the dogs love to race, they hate the crowds and noise. There are hundreds of thousands of people, cars, helicopters, and, above all else, noise. It makes the dogs jittery and the drivers tense. Fourth Street is where it all starts. At a banquet a couple of evenings before the race, you'll draw your starting position. Nine o'clock marks the ceremonial start of the race with the honorary number one racer send-off. After that, the race officially begins at nine-o-two. Racers will take off every two minutes after that, and during the ride to Eagle River you'll carry a passenger."

"That's you, Daddy," Rita said, offering August a smile. August couldn't help but return his daughter's gesture.

"Who's riding with you, Mark?" August questioned.

"I have a friend in Anchorage and I've

asked him to ride with me. It's kind of a pre-wedding present," Mark replied. "In fact, after the race, I'm going to be his best man."

"You never mentioned this, Mark," August commented with a quick glance at Rita. He noted the flash in her eyes that bespoke of sudden interest.

"I meant to. When I was arranging help for the kennel so that you and Beth could spend time in Anchorage, I arranged to cover the extra day I'd be away for the wedding. I was going to mention it to you the other day because I needed to pick up the wedding ring in Fairbanks, but you made it easy on me with that trip to town, and I just forgot."

Rita nearly fell off her chair. So the ring wasn't Mark's. This changed everything. But did she want it to? When she'd thought that Mark had someone else in his life, it was easier for Rita to separate her feelings from her thoughts.

Rita's reaction wasn't lost on August or Mark, but both men kept their thoughts to themselves, while Rita struggled just to hear what was being said about the trail.

February came quickly to an end and Rita found herself on the way to Anchorage with her father. Her mother was coming down with Gerald and his wife in order to join in the festivities. After the Iditarod started, they would drive the dog vehicles to Eagle River, where they would meet Rita and her team after the first leg of the race. At Eagle River, the dogs and sleds would be loaded into trucks and driven to Wasilla, where the entire race would start again. The trail in earlier years passed over the mudflats of upper Cook Inlet to Knik. Due to the hazards of this area, when unseasonable warmth left the ground and water unfrozen, the race was officially changed to restart in Wasilla.

The truck hit a series of bumps along a stretch of worn-out highway. Rita seemed not to notice. "I'm so excited, Dad."

"It only gets better," August said with a smile.

"I love the anticipation. Just knowing that something glorious like the Iditarod awaits is enough to keep me on the edge of my seat. I keep thinking of how it's going to be, and even though I've never been there, you and Mark have made me feel as if I know how it will be," Rita chattered.

August nodded. "I'm glad you're excited. I knew you would be. You're finally realizing your dream and that's something quite special. I'm grateful to be a part of it before I die."

"Don't talk about dying, Daddy." Rita's voice betrayed her fear.

"Rita, you don't need to worry about me. I'm not afraid to die; and when my time comes, I'll be ready. I guess my only real concern is whether or not you will be."

Rita swallowed hard. She thought of the verses her aunt Julie had shared and all of her mother's speeches. Somehow those things were easier to deal with than her father's worries.

August tried not to notice the way Rita paled. Death, particularly the possibility of his death, caused Rita a great deal of fear. "Rita," he began gently, "you must let go of the fear you feel inside. Trust isn't an easy thing, but trust in God is something that will never let you down, because God will never let you down."

"How can you be so sure?" Rita barely whispered the question.

"It's a matter of believing in the promises that God has given in the Bible, Rita. He said He'd never leave us and He never will."

"It's so hard," Rita replied. "The whole concept is difficult to believe. I mean, I see that God is real to you and Mom. I guess even Mark sees Him in a real way; but it just doesn't feel that way to me. I've prayed before, but I never felt as though my prayers went any farther than the room I was in. God just never made Himself very evident to me."

August nodded. "I can understand your predicament. I went through a time like that, too. Of course, you know all about that, and it isn't what's important right now. What is important is that you can have God in your life in a very real way. If you want Him, Rita, God will be there for you and He will help you to see Him."

"I'm afraid of trying." Rita's honest words hung in the air. "I mean, it seems like everyone I've ever cared about has deserted me. Everyone but you, that is."

"Do you really believe that?" August questioned.

"I don't know, Daddy. All I know is that ever since I was a little girl, I tried to understand why Mom felt so angry with me all the time and why none of my brothers or sisters seemed to have the time of day for me."

"Your brothers and sisters were all so much older than you. You turned out to be a surprise gift from the Lord. You have to remember that you came nearly nine years after we presumed we were finished with diapers and bottles. Nevertheless, we loved you as much as any of the rest," August replied.

Rita shook her head. "No, I don't think so. You may have felt that way, but Mother didn't. I overheard her tell Sarah that she'd never wanted me."

August looked stunned. "I find that hard to believe, Rita. I mean, I know the pregnancy was a shock to your mother and that we had to change a lot of plans, but I remember when she gave birth to you. I watched her nurse you. Your mother loved you as much as any of the others."

Rita winced and fell silent.

"Look, Rita," August said, dividing his concentration between the road and his daughter, "the issue here isn't the past, but the future. I'm going to pray that God will reveal Himself to you in a very real way and I'm going to pray that you can somehow get over your hurtful relationship with your mother and start over."

Rita looked out the window to avoid her father's face. She didn't want to appear vulnerable to his words, but the truth was, she felt compelled to listen.

"I mean it, Rita," August said in an authoritative voice. "I want you to figure out what the problem is between you and your mom and deal with it. I don't want to leave this world with the concern that either one of you is alone. I want you to be there for each other. I want you to love each other."

August's words hung on the air, stifling Rita into silent submission. *I want you to love each other,* resounded in her mind as the forested miles of highway ticked by.

Chapter 9

The noise at the starting line on Fourth Street was intense and nerve-racking. Rita stood beside her dogs, soothing, quieting, and rechecking every harness and line. She could feel the adrenaline surging through her veins, making her heart pound hard against her temples.

Mentally, she made a list of the items she'd packed, and one by one she went over them. With each crunch of snow beneath her heavy boots, Rita felt the urge to be off building inside.

Dandy gave a whimpered howl that was quickly followed by howls from the other dogs. Rita saw her father lean over and give the lead dog a quick pat on the head. She thought he whispered something to the dog, but found a tap on her shoulder distracted her from finding out what it was that August had said.

"Yes?" She whirled around to find Mark's intense eyes. His cheeks were red from the wind, but his expression of excitement matched her own.

"Are you ready, Texas Rita?" Mark asked in puffs of icy air.

Rita couldn't help but grin. "I feel like I've worked a lifetime to get here."

"You have worked hard," Mark agreed. "I'm proud of the way you put aside our differences."

Rita prickled at Mark's words. "I don't know what you're talking about."

Mark laughed. "You weren't the most cooperative student, as I recall."

Rita started to answer but found her reply interrupted by one of the race officials.

"I'm here to mark your dogs," he told her as he moved with paint to dab on each dog's fur for purposes of identification. This would prevent the switching of dogs while out on the trail. Rita anticipated this from things her father and Mark had told her; still she didn't like anyone else handling her dogs.

She followed the man in silence, however, her mind still on Mark's words. *Forget about him,* she chided her heart and mind. *You don't need him or anyone else*. Yet even as she tried to convince herself of this, her father's words of salvation and heavenly security kept pounding at her.

By the time the official moved on, Rita found Mark gone as well. August came up with a grin a mile wide.

"Okay Number Nineteen," he said, referring to the number Rita had drawn for her position in the start of the Iditarod, "it won't be long now."

"I know," Rita mumbled.

"What's wrong?" August asked, suddenly concerned.

"Umm? Oh, nothing," Rita said, noting her father's worried look. She wanted to assure him, but in order to keep her guard up, she also needed to distance herself. "It's just jitters, Dad."

"I understand. Look, we're going to be taking off shortly. Do you have everything?" August asked.

"I think so," Rita answered. "Where's Mom and Gerald?"

"Oh, they're out there, somewhere. Don't you worry about them. They'll be there at Eagle River waiting with the dog trucks."

"Well, I guess that's all I can ask," Rita said with a hesitant smile.

"Don't worry," August said as he patted his daughter's hand. "Everything will be fine once the race starts."

Rita wanted to believe that, but in her heart she knew the turmoil was about much more than the race.

"One more, Rita," August called from the sled basket. "One more racer and then we're off."

Rita said nothing. Her mind was a blur of fanatical fans waving and yelling their support. Where in the world had all those people come from? There were television cameras and reporters everywhere, not to mention five blocks of colorful, screaming people and extremely bright lights.

The next thing Rita knew was the numbing grip of her hand on the sled handle and the pounding of her heart in her ears.

"Nineteen — go!" the announcer called.

"Dandy, hike!" Rita yelled above the crowd's roar. Dandy led the pack of dogs without need of encouragement. The team was in a near frenzy as they shot down the street.

Rita knew nothing but the feel of the dogs and the frosty air against her cheeks. The sounds were all muted in her head while the faces blended into one.

I'm really doing it! Rita thought. *I'm finally racing the Iditarod!*

The race trail headed down Cordova Hill, with a spectacular view of downtown Anchorage. Rita worked to slow the team as they plunged down the slope, but the dogs were as excited as she was. It was exhilarating and no one wanted to slow down for any reason.

The next miles followed inner-city trails where people still cheered the mushers on. It wasn't until the trail finally began to parallel the Glenn Highway that the people thinned to sporadic gatherings.

"Isn't this great!" August yelled over his shoulder.

"Yes," Rita replied. "It's everything I knew it would be."

August laughed heartily. "You ain't seen nothin' yet, kid. Hang on for Act Two. It's a doozy!"

Amidst the noise of people and crowds, Rita worked hard to keep the team under control. Each time they approached an intersection, traffic was stopped from all directions while her team moved through, but the honking of zealous fans and general pandemonium made driving the team a tiresome task.

Rita had hoped to think through her anger and frustration on the trail, but if the run from Anchorage to Eagle River was any indication of how her time would be spent, there wouldn't be much time for thinking.

Two hours and eighteen minutes later, without a single mishap, Rita and August passed under the banner welcoming them to Eagle River.

"Good time, Rita," August said as they checked in.

Rita nodded and looked around for Mark. He'd left a good ten places behind her, but that didn't mean a great deal. She'd no sooner cast a squinted stare at the horizon when she caught sight of him. He was making incredible time.

August spotted him about the same time. "I bet he'll be under two hours!" The excitement in August's voice left a jealous mark on Rita's heart.

Mark came flying across the trail and clocked in at one hour and fifty-eight minutes. While August stomped off through the snow to congratulate his partner, Rita cooled her heels and unharnessed her dogs.

"You did well, Rita," her brother said as he came to help her with loading the animals.

"Thanks, Gerald. It's good to see you again," she answered rather mechanically, not really meaning a word she said. Rita knew it wasn't fair to take out her fury on Gerald, but she ignored her pang of conscience and kept her distance.

"Rita!" Beth called as she got out of the pickup. "What was your time?"

"Two-eighteen," Rita replied, surprised at her mother's enthusiasm.

"Fantastic!" Beth stepped forward and hugged her daughter. She laughed as she pulled away from Rita. "There's so much padding to you, I'm not at all convinced that you're really under all of that," she said, pointing to Rita's insulated coveralls.

Rita laughed in spite of herself. She'd never seen her mother so happy, especially when it involved Rita. Surprisingly enough, it was her father who spoiled Rita's moment of happiness.

"Mark did it in an hour and fifty-eight minutes!" said August. "Can you believe it, Beth?"

"That's great," Beth agreed. "I'm so proud of Rita and Mark. They've done really well, haven't they?" It was more a statement than a question.

"They certainly have," August said. "Now we need to get these animals loaded up and move up to Wasilla."

Rita felt disappointed in the lack of fanfare from her father. Somehow she'd presumed he'd been her biggest fan, not her mother. Putting it behind her, Rita knew she'd have plenty of time to contemplate it on the way to Wasilla.

The next day the whole thing started all over. This time Rita waited behind while Mark disappeared down the trail. In her mind was the overwhelming drive to beat his time and win the race.

For all the truly important reasons, Wasilla was where the Iditarod really began. The race restarted with the biggest difference being that this time the racers went out alone. Rita refused to even look back when her time came. When the signal was given, she steadied herself behind the sled and ran for all she was worth.

The first one hundred miles out of Wasilla was called "Moose Alley" and for a good reason. It was here that the race trail passed through an area where large numbers of moose spent the winter. When the snow became too deep for the moose to find food, they often took to the roadways, railroad tracks, and any place else that had been cleared of the blanket of white.

Rita kept alert for any interference and, in the process, passed two other teams who were already experiencing problems. She was out less than four hours when the snow began to fall. At first the flakes came down in gentle flurries, but within a matter of several miles, the conditions had built into a full-fledged blizzard. Rita came upon four teams who had backtracked their way in order to relocate the trail and, rather than lose her place and assure everyone they were headed in the right direction, Rita took a gamble and headed on.

The gamble paid off and Rita soon found one of the trail markers. "Good," she said aloud, adrenaline racing through her system. "I've moved out ahead of six teams already. If I'm just willing to take a few chances, I can win this race!"

When the snow let up a bit, Rita knew it would be a good time to rest the dogs. She pulled off the trail and dug out dried fish for each of the team. She felt hot inside her multiple layers of clothing, and it was then that she realized the temperatures were warming.

Glancing around her, Rita could see a clearing in the skies up ahead and bright sunlight filtering through the sporadic cloud coverage. The snow had stopped falling altogether, but the trail had been partially obliterated by the storm. In the far distance, Rita thought she heard dogs barking. Her pulse began to race. "I can't lose ground, now."

Rita resecured the sled cargo, shed her heavy parka, and pulled on a beaver fur hat that her mother had made for her as a Christmas gift. She pulled sunglasses from a pouch near the handle bar, stuffed them in her insulated coveralls, and pressed the dogs forward.

Rita believed luck was with her as the skies cleared and the trail markers appeared faithfully. She urged the dogs to go faster and faster, but they slowed as the trail grew mushy from the sun's warmth.

Rethinking her strategy, Rita reasoned that waiting for sunset might be better for her time and the dogs' health. She drove them another couple of hours and finally located a place near a stream. Her mind whirled as she rationalized her decision.

"Everyone will be slowed down by the thawing trail," she spoke to herself. "No one will make good time, and if I stop now, rest and feed the dogs and take a nap myself, we'll be able to push through all night." It was sensible, but with each team that passed her, Rita felt the urge to get back behind the sled and join them.

Instead, Rita built a fire and heated food for the dogs. After seeing each of them fed and bedded down, she pulled out her heavy snow parka and laid down on top of her sled. Setting the alarm on her watch for four o'clock, Rita placed the timepiece in her fur hat so that it was right up against her ear. Then, pulling the parka over her body and face, Rita slept.

Again the gamble paid off. When Rita awoke, the sunlight was fading and the trail was already growing firm again. After making sure to water the dogs one more time to keep them from trying to eat snow on the trail, Rita moved out for her next checkpoint — Skwenta, Alaska.

When she arrived at the checkpoint, most of the teams had been there far ahead of her. Some of the drivers were giving their dogs extra rest; but as soon as Rita checked in, she felt like hitting the trail again. The Delia House, long known for its hospitality, held a welcome aroma of chili, stews, and freshly brewed coffee.

Rita sat down nervously to a bowl of beef stew and bread while she mentally calculated who was who and what kind of time they must have maintained. She gulped the food down. While most of the other drivers went to sleep, Rita donned her parka again and went back to her dogs.

The one thing she hadn't counted on was a deluge of reporters. Flashbulbs went off, making the dogs nervous and blinding Rita.

"You're not pushing out again, are you?" one reporter asked and thrust a tape recorder in front of Rita.

"Y–yes," Rita stammered and tried to shield her eyes from the television camera lights that were added to the flashing lights.

"The other drivers are giving their dogs a longer rest. Aren't you concerned that your dogs will be overworked?" a woman interviewer questioned. "I thought there were strict rules about the dogs."

"I rested early in the day when the trails were mushy. My dogs are fine," Rita replied in clipped tones that betrayed her agitation. "Now, if you'll excuse me."

Rita hurried to leave the checkpoint, and after meeting all her obligations, quickly found her way down the trail and headed for Finger Lake.

In the bright moonlight, the trail was easy enough. The stars filled the skies overhead, and Rita thought she'd never known anything as beautiful. Following the Skwenta River, Rita calculated that Finger Lake was some forty-five miles away. She knew she'd have to rest the dogs for short spells before then, but Finger Lake would represent her next major stop.

Silently, she watched the miles pass by. She saw the heavy cloud bank that edged its way across the western skies, while over her right shoulder northern lights danced in the March sky. What a land of contrast!

Lowlands gave way to foothills and foothills passed into the mighty Alaskan Range. Even though each passing mile offered more difficult obstacles, one thought haunted Rita's mind — *Where was Mark and what kind of time was he keeping?*

Chapter 10

The following day wasn't quite as warm, but Rita repeated her system between intermittent snows. She knew that other drivers were following the same plan, and she kept moving as quickly as possible to gain distance.

True to what her father and Mark had told her, she couldn't count more than a few hours of sleep in total. The lack of sleep didn't discourage her, however. Rita kept reminding herself of how easy the trail had been so far and, despite her desperate need for sleep, she kept to her self-appointed schedule.

"I've taken chances," she said aloud, "but they've paid off and I know they were the right things to do."

Rita smiled to herself as the dogs moved at a steady lope. At Finger Lake she'd moved up nine places, and after an uneventful roller coaster ride through Happy River Gorge, Rita was beginning to feel smug in her self-confidence. "I knew I didn't need anybody," she reminded herself. The cold wind made her cheekbones numb, but she didn't care. She knew she could win the race.

In the back of her mind, August's words mingled with her self-assured thoughts. Her father said she needed God and no matter how she tried to deny Him, Rita knew it was true. That was the biggest problem about all the miles of solitude on the trail — it gave a person too much time to think.

Rita thought about stopping the dogs in order to get her headphones. Maybe listening to some of her favorite music would help her to keep her conscience in check. She glanced at her watch and decided against it. She could just as well block out the thoughts by forcing her interests elsewhere. At least, she hoped she could.

The dogs were holding up well, and each checkpoint had shown them to be in excellent shape despite the way Rita pushed them. It was Rita who suffered. At times she thought she imagined teams just ahead of her, but when she rubbed her eyes with the back of her mittens, the images faded.

It wasn't until Rita thought the dogsled was floating up into the air that she decided to rest. Rohn was only a few hours ahead of her and both Mark and her father had suggested she spend her twenty-four-hour layover there. All she had to do was hold on until Rohn.

While Rohn and a good night's sleep waited just down the trail, Rita knew she would still have to face the challenge of Dalzell Gorge. Her father had described this stretch of the Iditarod as a nightmare.

First, there was the climb from Puntilla Lake to 3,200-foot Rainy Pass. The dogs had managed this with relative ease, and Rita was beginning to think they were living a charmed life. Maybe her father had just been overly tired by the time he'd come this far, she surmised. Maybe it was just that he was so much older when he'd run the race.

As the team crossed over the divide, Rita had to turn her full attention to the trail at hand. The path ahead plunged into a steep, winding trail that moved rapidly downhill at a rate of about one thousand feet in little more than five miles.

Rita clung to the bar and rode the brake constantly to counter the dogs' continued slipping. At one point she saw Dandy go down and slide several feet. Over and over the dogs recovered their falls while Rita found herself near to prayer for the safety of the team.

Things went better for several minutes and Rita breathed a sigh of relief. She tried to get her bearings on the situation, feeling her pulse racing wildly. Ahead of her, the narrow canyon was lined with boulders and crossed several ice bridges that spanned partially frozen creeks. If the dogs lost their footing while traveling over the bridges, they could send the entire team, sled and all, into the water below. Rita couldn't afford to lose the time, nor would she endanger the dogs.

"Dandy, whoa!" she called and held the brake tight to bring the dogs to a near stop. Easing them forward, Rita held her breath with each crossing and didn't let it out until they'd safely reached the opposite side.

"Just get us to Rohn," Rita murmured, uncertain to whom she was speaking. "We'll be fine if we can just get to Rohn."

The shelter cabin at Rohn waited as official Iditarod Checkpoint Number Eight. Rita dragged into the clearing running behind the sled on nothing but sheer determination. She was now two hundred seventy-five miles from Anchorage and, while the halfway mark was still to be reached, Rita was simply grateful for having made it this far.

Coming to a halt, Rita was quickly surrounded by people. One by one she answered questions and even signed an autograph book, before the crowd dispersed and left her to work.

"I see you're still in one piece." It was Mark.

Rita cast a weary glance upward from where she had bent down to check over her dogs. "You, too," was all that squeaked out.

"You gonna layover here?" Mark asked sympathetically.

"Yes." Rita straightened out and nearly fell over.

"Easy," Mark said, reaching out to steady her.

"I'm fine, really," Rita answered and tried to push away. "I have to log in and let them know I'm staying." She started to walk away but turned back around. "What about you?"

"I'll be leaving in a few hours," Mark replied. The concern he held for Rita was evident in his expression.

"You're that far ahead of me?"

"Is that all that concerns you?" Mark asked a bit sarcastically.

Rita rolled her neck to relieve the strain. "It isn't everything, but it's important."

Mark shook his head as Rita moved off to speak to the officials. He knew it was difficult to truly enjoy the race while you were running it, but in Rita's case it was even worse. She was all driving competition and no pleasure. The fire of that drive was clear in her eyes, in spite of her exhaustion.

Rita tried to ignore the way Mark stared after her. She met her race responsibilities, picked up supplies, and moved away from the shelter area to bed down with the dogs.

"The wind's due to pick up tonight," Mark said from somewhere behind her.

Rita turned wearily to find him toting a bale of straw. "What are you doing?"

"Just bringing the dogs some bedding." His casual reply left Rita no room to protest.

"What's the temperature?" she asked instead and reached into her pocket for a knife to cut the baling wire.

"Thirty below and dropping. When that wind comes down the pass, it's going to feel like a hundred below. I'd climb in that sled and in my sleeping bag if I were you," Mark answered.

"Just put the bale here," she motioned. "I'm going to stake out the dogs and then I'll distribute the straw." Mark dropped the bale and stood back wishing he could do more to ease Rita's exhaustion. He knew she needed to do everything for herself, but he also knew her pride wouldn't allow her to think rationally.

"May I keep you company while you get the dogs fed and watered?" he questioned.

"I guess so," Rita said and moved painfully slowly to position her dogs.

No other conversation passed between them until after Rita had a hearty fire roaring. She thawed rich mixtures of commercial dog food, liver, chicken, and salmon to feed the dogs, then melted snow and poured water for each one until she was certain they'd had their fill. Mark made conversation that was solely responsible for keeping Rita on her feet, but she never would have admitted his help.

"You gonna eat?" Mark asked when he saw that Rita was finished with the dogs.

"No," she sighed. A gust of wind blew through the trees just then. "It's getting colder and I'm going to sleep. Will I see you when I wake up?"

"I doubt it. You won't surface dreamland for ten or twelve hours if my guess is right. I'll be gone in two."

Rita nodded. She wanted to ask him about his time, but her mind begged for sleep. "I'll see you when you cross the finish line in Nome, then." Her reply amused Mark.

"Not likely, Eriksson. Not likely."

Rita watched Mark walk away. She hadn't realized how comforting his presence was until he stood in the lighted doorway of the Bureau of Land Management cabin and turned to offer her a wave before going inside.

Stripping off her parka and wet coveralls, Rita quickly pulled the sleeping bag around her and nuzzled down into the sled basket. She wiggled around to work the sled cover up over her before burying her head inside the sleeping bag. The warmth eased her aching muscles and sleep was immediate. For the first time in days, Rita gave in to the demands of her body.

When Rita awoke nine hours later, she could hear the wind howling from outside her sled bag. She pulled her wristwatch to her face and hit the light button to reveal the date and time. Seeing that she was still early into her twenty-four hours, Rita allowed herself to linger in the warmth.

Licking her lips slowly, Rita realized for the first time how cracked and dried they were. Water sounded even better than food, and her stomach was protesting quite loudly for that substance. It was a difficult choice. Food and water or restful warmth?

Finally choosing the food, Rita pushed back the basket cover and peered out. During the night, the winds had brought snow and buried the dogs and the basket in an insulation of white. Rita pulled her frozen coveralls on and secured her parka, while Dandy lazily peeked blue eyes out from where his bushy tail covered his muzzle.

"Well, boy," Rita called out. "What do you think? Are we going to win this race?" Dandy whimpered, then yipped. "I'll take that as a yes," Rita answered and went to work melting snow.

By the time Rita's layover was completed, the wind had picked up to forty miles an hour and the temperature registered at forty-five below. Thick, heavy snow clouds hung in a gray lifeless form over the entire area. There would be little, if any, light today, Rita surmised.

She quickly harnessed the dogs and

stood ready to leave when her official twenty-four hours was up. It was almost like starting the race again. The dogs were refreshed, well fed and watered, and eager for the trail. They lived to do this work and they loved it. Rita smiled as she stroked Dandy one last time, remembering a woman in Anchorage who thought it cruel that Rita raced her dogs. The woman couldn't understand. She saw the harnesses of confinement and the weight of the load. What she didn't see was the animation in the dogs, their yips of enthusiasm, their jumps of excitement. Nor did this woman know of the dogs left behind to howl and mourn their misfortune. It was all a matter of how one looked at the situation.

Something in Rita's heart took notice at that thought. Her mother's indifference came to mind. Rita frowned at the memory and quickly brushed it aside. A matter of perspective or not, Rita had a race to run and now wasn't the time for soul-searching. Or was it?

The trail was firm beneath her feet as Rita ran behind her sled. The dogs, ever faithful to their job, kept a steady lope as they moved out of the Rohn area and past the Kuskokwim River's south fork. Rita had been thoroughly warned about the trail to come. She would soon be passing into the Farewell Burn. This 360,000-acre area of tundra and spruce forests had been destroyed many years prior in a forest fire. It left behind an obstacle course of fallen trees and regrowth of sedge-tussock tundra. The tussock, clumps of grass that mushroomed out two feet high or more, froze solid in the winter and presented rock-solid opposition to the racers of the Iditarod. Many a driver had been injured, some even seriously, when their sleds and teams had run up against the tussock.

Rita calculated the checkpoints to come. There would be Nikolai first, then McGrath, Takotna, and finally Ophir. Ophir was where the trail would separate and take the southerly route and pass through Iditarod and it was Iditarod that represented the halfway mark. It seemed like a whole world away.

The hours rushed by and the distance passed, too. Rita had found the "Burn" painfully tedious and slow. Snow made visibility difficult, but, one by one, Rita located the trail markers and pressed on. The checkpoints passed quickly, and with them came the cultural change from areas that had been heavily influenced by the whites to lands primarily settled with native Athapaskan Indians.

She was greeted enthusiastically at Nikolai, finding herself in fifth position, but still behind Mark. The villagers had greeted each arriving team with shouts of praise and welcome. A huge bonfire had been built for the purpose of heating water for the dogs, and the school had been dismissed to allow the children to run from team to team seeking autographs.

Rita was given a hot meat sandwich that she quickly wolfed down before pushing on. Leaving a single sled team behind while the driver changed runners, Rita pushed ahead for McGrath.

By nightfall she'd made Takotna. This river town had served as a landing and supply center during the gold rush days in Alaska. Now only numbering around fifty in population, Rita was welcomed every bit as heartily as she had been in Nikolai. She'd never seen so much food in all her life and graciously ate her fill after seeing to it that her team ate first.

The snow fell heavier still as she mushed out to reach Ophir. More than one native encouraged her to stay on in Takotna until the storm abated, but Rita was feverish with the thought of passing Mark.

It was the endless miles of darkness that gave Rita too much time to think. "If I can only make it to Iditarod first," she whispered to the night skies, "I could win the silver ingots and give them to Dad." There are only five teams in front of me and one of them is Mark, she thought to herself and disregarded the beliefs that being the first one to reach the halfway point jinxed you from winning the race. She knew that only once had the midway winner gone on to win the Iditarod, but she simply didn't care. She wished there were some way to slow down the other teams.

When she finally arrived in Ophir, amidst near-blizzard conditions, Rita felt as though she'd been granted her wish. All five of the teams ahead of her, including Mark's, were still there.

Mark met her and noted the frenzied excitement in her eye. "The weather's too bad to push ahead," Mark commented as Rita's team approached him. "We've decided to hold up a spell."

"Have they put a freeze on the race?" Rita questioned, feeling her fervor fade.

"No," Mark replied. "We just know what these storms are like. It'll blow over in a short time and we can be off then. There's no use in risking life and limb."

"I can't believe you're all afraid to go out in this," Rita said, waving her hand. "I've come the last twenty miles in this storm and, while cold and extremely frustrating, it's not worth stopping for."

"You don't mean that you plan to move on out in it?" Mark's question fanned the flame of Rita's pride.

"I certainly do. As soon as I get the team cared for, we're out of here." She hurried off before Mark could say anything to stop her. There was a chance to win the ingots. There was a chance to win the race!

Chapter 11

"I don't want you to go, Rita," Mark stated. He put his hand out to take hold of Dandy's harness. "I owe it to your father to keep you from risking your life out there."

Rita's eyes blazed holes in Mark's heart. "Let go of my dogs. It's my choice to run, just as it was your choice to stay. My father isn't out here running this race, I am. Now let me go."

Mark dropped the harness and took hold of Rita with both hands. "It's suicide to go any farther," Mark tried to reason. "If you don't care about your family, I do. I don't want to have to explain to them how I allowed you to go out and become the first human life lost in the entire history of the Iditarod."

"I never asked you to babysit me," Rita said in a surprisingly calm tone.

"I just care about you, Rita. Think about

it. I think I've proven it enough times. It's not just August and Beth. I care about what happens to you."

Rita felt her resolve giving way; her eyes softened for a moment before she shrugged away from Mark's hold. "I don't want you to care," she whispered and walked back to the sled. She gave a soft whistle barely heard through the wind, but it was enough that Dandy's sensitive ears picked it up and then they were gone.

Mark kicked at the snow and muttered all the way back to where his team was contentedly curled up beneath the snow. He began to ready his sled without real thought to what he was doing, but in his heart he knew that he'd have to follow Rita. He'd never forgive himself if something happened to her.

"Williams!" a voice sounded above the wind. "Where are you going?" It was one of the checkpoint officials.

"I'm heading out for Iditarod," Mark replied.

"I can't let you go," the man returned. "They've put a freeze on the race. Can't get supplies flown up to the next checkpoints because of the blizzard. Until they can, the race stops."

"But Rita Eriksson just left a few minutes ago. She'll be out there all alone if I don't follow her," Mark protested, even knowing how foolish his argument sounded.

"Sorry, Williams. She took off before the word came down, but if you head out, you'll be breaking the rules." The man saw the look of concern on Mark's face. "It shouldn't be a long wait. Try not to worry."

But it was a long wait, and team after team arrived in Ophir only to be told they had to stay put until supplies could be sent on ahead. Most took the opportunity to sleep or repair their sleds, but Mark paced and fretted until he was nearly sick from the thought of Rita meeting with an accident.

"Lord," Mark found himself praying, "I don't understand what gets into that woman, but I care for her in a way I wasn't sure I could ever care for another human being. Lord, I don't want her to die and yet . . ." His words trailed into silence as he remembered a sermon he'd once heard about people thwarting God's efforts to work in the lives of rebellious souls. "God, I don't want to interfere in Your plans for Rita. Go with her and help me to leave it in

Your hands, Amen."

The prayer made Mark feel marginally better, but when one day passed into two and the checkpoint official gave him the news that Rita had never made it to Iditarod, Mark could stand it no longer.

"I have to go after her!" he said as he readied his dogs.

"You'll just get yourself killed," the official told him. "Or, you'll be disqualified from the race."

"I don't care. I'm a certified search and rescue team member. I can't just sit here knowing that she's out there somewhere in this storm. I have to try to find her, or I'm afraid she's not going to come out of this alive. Do you really want to be the one remembered for keeping a racer from being saved?"

"I'll send out other people," the man replied. "I assure you, Miss Eriksson will be located as soon as possible, but I can't risk the lives of ten other people because of the foolish gamble of one racer."

"I'm not asking you to," Mark said, taking hold of the sled bar. "I'll gladly give my own life for hers."

The man's face changed from angry frustration to confusion. Mark took the man's silence as a form of understanding and pushed the dogs out into the storm.

Rita knew she was hopelessly lost. She hadn't been able to locate a marker or tag of any kind and the trail was long since obliterated.

The blizzard raged on around her, making it impossible to care for the dogs or even set up a proper camp. The few times she'd tried, she'd failed miserably and struggled to push on. When the wind let up a bit, she strained to hear the sounds of civilization. Nothing came back to her ears but the deathlike silence. Exhaustion hung round her like a mantle of fur.

"I've got to make camp. I've got to rest," she said aloud. The dogs were wearing out fast, and Rita knew she was pushing them dangerously close to dehydration and death.

Feeling her way along the team, Rita checked the dogs' feet. She needed to change the booties on two of the dogs' paws. She hated this job that, even under good circumstances, was difficult to do. Each dog represented four booties and four dancing paws, and Rita would have to discard her mittens and gloves because it was impossible to put the tiny socks on and get the closures secured through padded fingers.

The exposure to windchills of minus one hundred degrees could freeze flesh in a matter of seconds, and Rita knew the only way to combat the cold would be to pull her gloves off and on for each bootie.

"This isn't fair," she screamed to the howling wind. "I deserve to win this race. I've taken the chances. I've sacrificed my comfort. Why are You against me, God?"

A blast of wind slammed into Rita, knocking her into the team. The dogs yipped and tangled, while she fought the harnesses and lines to recover from the fall. She felt tears form and just as quickly they froze to her lashes and burned her eyes.

"What is it You want of me, Lord? I can't go back. I can't go forward. If You won't help me," Rita moaned, "why must You hurt me?"

Rita crawled on her hands and knees to get back to the sled basket. Each inch covered was filled with pain, but Rita was determined to make it. She managed to open the covering even though she couldn't see it through the snow and her painful eyes.

Now the worst was upon her. Rita knew she would have to shed her wet clothes if she was to ever gain warmth in her sleeping bag. With nearly frozen fingers, Rita placed her mittens inside the basket and worked her way out of the layers of clothes. At the first possible moment, she scurried into the sleeping bag and snuggled down into the basket.

Mark knew his plan was foolish, yet he also knew he maintained an edge of experience that Rita didn't have. He and his team had been in situations like this before and would no doubt be in them again.

Wind and snow pelted them as Mark led the team forward at a steady walk. Moving slowly and working his way diligently, Mark managed to find the first marker without too much difficulty. He reassured the dogs with praise and pressed on. All the while he looked for anything that would indicate that Rita had passed through the same area.

Pausing in the storm, Mark lifted up a prayer. "Please Lord, help me in this search. You know where Rita is and You can guide me to her. Please abate this storm, in the name of Jesus. Amen."

Mark kept moving. Through the blowing snow he constantly had to break trail for the dogs. He felt the exhaustion of hours spent in snowshoes rapidly draining his strength. Just when he thought he'd have to turn back, a miracle happened — the snow stopped.

"Thanks, God," Mark whispered under his breath.

Rita finally felt her body begin to thaw and, with the warmth, she was able to think more clearly. Her first order of business had to be caring for the dogs. She could hear the wind howling outside the sled basket, in fact, it rocked the sled as she lay inside. No doubt the dogs had curled up to sleep and were now buried beneath a layer of snow, oblivious to the perils at hand. Rita wished silently that she could be as incognizant.

Shifting her weight, Rita pushed back her fur hat and moaned. A painful knot had formed on her forehead from where she'd hit it when the wind knocked her to the ground. Rita knew she wasn't seriously wounded, but her head was pounding as her body warmed.

"I guess my charmed portion of the trip is over," Rita mused. She tried to encourage her weary heart, but it was difficult at best. Were she in the habit of prayer, she might consider talking things over with God, but that wasn't her style. In the back of her mind, however, Rita couldn't help but think of a hundred different Bible stories where people found themselves facing problems and hardships. Memory verses from childhood reminded her of their commitment to God and how they cried out to Him when they were in trouble.

"Mother would like this," Rita laughed. "She's always pushing God at me. Now here I am in the middle of Alaska, in a blizzard, without a clue as to where I am, and all I can focus on is how God helped people in the Bible."

Rita felt the sled still and the wind grow calm. The storm was finally abating, and Rita knew it was time to get to work.

Pushing out of her cocoon, she crawled from the basket and surveyed the damage.

Dry, drifting snow still swirled in tiny whirlwinds around the sled, while Rita pulled on her insulated clothes and went into action to get a fire going. The exhausted dogs barely stirred, although Dandy raised his head to give Rita an appraising look before going back to sleep.

Within an hour she had food and water for both the dogs and herself. The skies overhead had cleared to a pale, powder blue. Even with the sun hanging above the southern horizon, there was little warmth. At least Rita could get her bearings now and hopefully relocate the trail. Her optimism returned and her heart grew lighter. The dogs, sensing the change in their mistress, grew excited again. They were pacing and yipping, and Rita knew they were ready to be back on the trail. But where was the trail?

Rita pulled on her snowshoes and led the dogs out. There was no clear direction that beckoned Rita more than another. She looked for anything that might indicate civilization or symbolize a connection with the Iditarod race, but there wasn't anything. She pulled out her compass and depended on it alone to guide her in a direction that would lead them to safety.

Hours later, the biggest mistake Rita had made was, once again, ignoring the weather. The snow moved in from the west and with it came the wind.

Old snow blew with the new, and soon Rita found it again impossible to see. The dogs whined and slowed, and Rita felt her courage slipping away. She halted the team and tied a rope to the sled and to herself. Using her headlamp, Rita left the dogs behind and ventured ahead to find some sign of shelter.

"I can't give up," she said, even though she knew she was now several days behind the other teams. She had no way of knowing that the other racers had just been allowed to leave Ophir.

Finding nothing to aid her on her way, Rita turned around and headed back to the dogs. She retraced her steps following the rope, and then she felt her heart skip a beat. The rope had come untied; the sled was nowhere in sight!

Chapter 12

Cold permeated the insulation of Rita's coveralls. She stomped aimlessly through the blowing snow, watching, calling, and hoping.

"Dandy!" she yelled at the top of her lungs, but the wind muted the sound even as the word left her lips.

The dogs were nowhere to be found and visibility was impossible. Rita knew the seriousness of the circumstances. Without the dogs, she would most likely die!

"I have to keep moving," she reasoned. "I'll freeze to death if I stand here and wait." She thought of building a shelter with the snow. Her aunt Julie told her that once such a shelter had saved her life. Rita remembered that her aunt Julie had survived two days just off the Bering Sea in a haven she'd built with her own hands out of snow and ice.

"No!" Rita spoke aloud. "I'll find the dogs. Dandy would never have left without me." But, even as she said the words, Rita knew it was improbable that the team was awaiting her return.

Step after step, Rita forced herself forward. Her feet were beginning to ache and her legs were cramping from the strain. It was fast becoming a hopeless situation.

After what seemed hours, Rita was ready to face the facts. "I'm not going to make it," she whispered. "I'm going to die out here doing the one thing I dreamed a lifetime of doing. All I wanted was to race the Iditarod and now it's going to kill me."

But running the race wasn't all, Rita's conscience quickly reminded her. Winning the race was what you planned on. Winning was so important that you ignored the advice of seasoned racers, people who knew the trail and have more experience than you could ever hope to have.

"I've been extremely foolish," Rita said and stumbled forward another step. Her thick boot caught the edge of a fallen tree and sent her sprawling, face down, onto the snowy ground.

Why get up? She challenged herself to find a reason to go on. There was none.

"This is God's punishment for ignoring Him and turning away from my mother," she announced. She had never felt so alone.

The thought of her mother made Rita's heart ache. All her life she'd wanted to feel close to Beth and, in spite of the times Rita had determined to put her hurts aside, inevitably, she added another brick to the wall between them.

"When times are difficult and you are most alone," her mother had told her, "God is no farther away than a whispered prayer."

The wind lessened and with it the snow, but Rita couldn't see anything but white. A whispered prayer came to Rita's mind, but not of her own making. The prayer she remembered was one from her childhood memories. It was her mother's prayer at Rita's bedside that came to mind. "Father, this child was given to me from You and by Your love. I give her back. Watch over her, Father, as only You can, and help her to know Your voice when You call her."

Such a sweet, yet simple prayer, Rita thought, and the memory warmed her. Nothing to offend or harm, only a mother's desire for her child to know God. The memory wasn't painful, it was pleasant, and Rita wondered silently how she could have allowed such hatred to grow against others, especially her mother.

Rita struggled to sit up and pulled her knees tightly to her chest. "I'm afraid to die," she whispered. "I know the truth, just like Mother said. I know what God did for me by sending His Son, Jesus, to die for me. I've always wanted God to somehow make Himself real to me. Yet, even sitting here waiting to die, He still doesn't seem real and I'm not convinced He'd listen to me even if I whispered that prayer." Absentmindedly, Rita began packing snow around herself to form a shelter.

Mark saw the reprieve in the storm as a godsend, but he also noticed the heavy clouds that pushed in from the west. The air was strangely still around him, and Mark found the silence almost hypnotic.

He urged his team forward, but knew he'd lost track of the trail markers some time back. "God, give me the wisdom to find my way through this. Guide me to find Rita and safety, Amen."

Just then a blurred image in the distance came into focus. It was a dog team. No, Mark realized as he squinted his eyes, it was Rita's dog team!

Having worked with those dogs since they were pups, Mark gave Dandy a whistle that the dog instantly recognized. "Here Dandy, come," Mark's authoritative voice called.

Dandy perked his ears and heeded the command. Mark anchored his own team and stomped across the frozen ground to retrieve Rita's team. He searched the horizon for Rita but found no one following the team, not even at a distance. Maybe she was in the basket, injured or sick, he reasoned. But when he finally brought the team up even with his own, Mark could see that Rita was not with them.

"Where is she, Dandy?" Mark questioned, giving the dog a rub on the muzzle. Dandy gave a yip, as if trying to answer the question.

"I wish you could talk," Mark sighed. "I'd best feed you all instead and then we'll push on to find Rita."

The delay cost Mark precious time, but he knew that the dogs had to be cared for. He piggybacked the sleds and harnessed Rita's dogs to run with his own. All the while, Mark kept eyeing the skies and the ominous clouds that threatened his success.

When Mark finally put out once again to look for Rita, light was fading quickly. He scrutinized the trees for any sign that Rita might be nearby. There was nothing.

Mark was losing hope when flakes of snow began to fall. "God, please help me!" he called out. Just then Dandy yipped and followed it with a deep throaty howl. Mark halted the dogs and watched Dandy's actions. The dog strained in his harness and pulled to the right as if he planned to pull the entire team with him if necessary.

Mark turned the team and brought Dandy to the lead. "Take us to Rita, boy," he urged. "Find her for me."

Dandy began barking in urgency then. He knew what Mark expected of him and was more than willing to respond to the call. Mark moved the dogs out and allowed Dandy to choose the course. Within moments, Mark spotted something red in the distance. Rita had worn red coveralls. It had to be her.

When he got closer, Mark began to panic. She wasn't moving or acknowledging his calls. "Please God, don't let her die," Mark whispered.

Mark anchored the team and hurried forward to where Rita sat in a tight ball. She'd obviously tried to pack a wall of snow around her. "Rita!" he called, and knelt down to push back her parka hood.

"Cold," Rita whimpered. "So cold."

Mark pulled her close and Rita moaned in agony. "Don't you go dying on me, Texas Rita." Mark tried to drawl good-naturedly. "Otherwise, you'll never see Texas, where the sun shines all the time and it's never cold."

Mark knew he was babbling, but his mind couldn't accept the possibility of Rita being anything other than healthy and strong. Hurrying back to the sled, Mark pulled out Rita's sleeping bag and his own as well. He brought both to where Rita had still not moved and began to work to get her wet parka off.

"Listen to me, Rita," he said as he unzipped her coveralls. "I've got to get these wet things off of you. Hopefully, the clothes beneath your coveralls are dry. When we finish with this, I'll put you inside the sleeping bags. Do you understand?"

"I understand," Rita whispered.

Mark wasn't convinced. "What do you understand, Rita? Tell me what I said."

"You're going to put me in the sleeping bag," she said in an irritable tone, "and you didn't call me Texas Rita."

Mark grinned. She still had fight left in her. He wasn't too late!

"What about my dogs? I lost my team," Rita mumbled.

"Dandy found me," Mark answered. "They're safe and in good shape. I only hope we can say the same thing about you."

Mark knew that once he had Rita inside the bags, he'd have more time to set up a proper camp. He was one of those few racers who liked to have a tent along in case of an emergency, and this time, it served its purpose well. He put Dandy with Rita before going to work.

Camp was set up in record time. Mark soon had the tent up, with a hearty fire glowing in the cookstove. The time would have been even shorter had he not run back and forth to check on Rita.

"The tent's ready," Mark said as he lifted Rita in his arms. "I'm going to put you inside and then I'll get you something hot to drink."

Rita said nothing until Mark had deposited her inside the tent; then, with teeth chattering, she thanked him. "Mark, I don't know how you managed to find me, but I'm glad you did."

"Me, too," Mark said and reached out to

touch Rita's frostbitten cheek. "You have no idea."

Then Mark went to get the hot coffee. When he returned with it, Rita wasn't sure she could even handle the cup. She felt as though her hands were on fire as they thawed, and her mind still seemed blurred.

"Drink it down and I'll make you some soup. I've got packages of dried-chicken noodle," he said with a grin. "Isn't that supposed to be a cure-all?"

Rita smiled even though it hurt to do so. The skin on her face felt tight, as though it might pull apart at the slightest movement. "I think it'll take more than chicken soup to cure what ails me."

Mark nodded. "I told you not to go out. I wish for once in your life you would have swallowed your pride and realized that sometimes others know best."

"I know I was wrong," Rita admitted. "I know it only too well."

"Well, this is a different side of you," Mark commented in surprise.

"Some people have to make their own foolish mistakes before they realize what fools they are. I guess I was one of those." Gone from Rita's voice was the severity and aloof reserve. "I just wanted to win the race. I wanted to show everyone that I could do it . . . that I didn't need anyone looking out for me."

"And now?" Mark questioned.

"Now, I know better," Rita replied. "I was scared to die, Mark. Not because I would never see Mom or Dad, or even you. . . ." She fell silent for a moment. "I didn't know what would happen. I didn't know where I would go or what death would really mean. I kept thinking about the Bible and the stories I'd learned as a child and a teenager. I thought of my mother's lectures on needing to be saved from my sins and I thought of what my father told me on the way to Anchorage."

"What was that?" Mark asked with a feeling he knew what Rita would say.

"Dad said, 'Rita, you must let go of the fear you feel inside.' He told me, 'Trust isn't an easy thing, but trust in God is something that will never let you down, because God will never let you down.' "

"Did you believe him?" Mark's face was stern, but his eyes were soft and warm.

"Not then," answered Rita.

"But what about now?"

"Now I realize I've been living on fear most all of my life. It's become such a part of my nature to distrust that I never saw the way it controlled me." Rita paused and looked thoughtfully at the cup in her hand before setting it aside.

"It's easy for other things to control us," Mark assured. "Things creep in that way and, before we realize it, we've become their victims. God's control isn't that way. He wants us to recognize Him as the controller. He wants us to see that He's in charge and find comfort in that fact."

Rita nodded. "I suppose I can see that now, but I've always been so independent." Outside, the wind picked up and moaned through the trees. "Even now, I'm skeptical. Not of God," she added at the look of bewilderment on Mark's face. "I'm skeptical that I can hand over the reins to my life and trust God to lead me."

"Do you want that, Rita?" Mark's question pierced Rita's heart.

From somewhere in Rita's memory, she began to quote Philippians 3:10–11. " 'I want to know Christ and the power of his resurrection and the fellowship of sharing in his sufferings, becoming like him in his death, and so, somehow, to attain to the resurrection from the dead.' "

"Truly, Rita? Do you want to accept Christ as your Savior?"

Rita hesitated only a moment. She didn't want to commit to God out of a sense of fear, yet wasn't she supposed to fear hell and eternal damnation? "I want to know about the love," she whispered, with tears falling freely from her eyes. "I know about the fear and the pain of rejection, but I want to know about the love."

Mark's heart nearly broke for her. She was so vulnerable and childlike that he moved from his spot and put his arms around her. "God is love, Rita. I know you're familiar with that verse if you can quote Philippians."

Rita nodded and tried to wipe away her tears. "I think it's the first verse I memorized as a small girl."

"It's true," Mark continued. "God is love and He demonstrated His love for us in sending Christ to take our punishment. He doesn't want you to come only out of fear; after all, the Israelites feared Him long before He sent Christ to them. He wanted to draw His people to Him, to show them His merciful love and eternal devotion. God loves His children, Rita. He loves you and He wants you to love Him."

"I do," Rita sobbed. "I always have, but my pride made me fear it. I just didn't want to get hurt again." She cried freely, unashamed of the tears.

Mark held her in silence until she was

spent. When Rita finally lifted her face, her eyes were gentler than Mark had ever known them.

"Are you and God at peace now, Rita?"

"Yes," Rita replied. "I know Jesus says that He's the only way to come to God. I know the Bible well, I've just never lived by it. I've asked God to forgive me, Mark, but I don't believe for one minute that life will all of a sudden be wonderful and perfect. I've a great deal of my past to put right."

"What past?" Mark asked with a grin. "You're a new creation in Christ, right? You've sought forgiveness for all those sins and the Bible says God remembers them no more."

"Yes, but people aren't God and people remember them," Rita countered.

"People aren't responsible for your salvation, Rita." Mark drove his point home. "God is the one you answer to. God is the one who will clear the way for you to mend fences with others. Trust Him, Rita. He can handle the job."

Rita put her head upon Mark's shoulder, enjoying the comfort of another. "I know you're right, but I'm still afraid."

"There's a verse in Psalm Fifty-six just for you. It says, 'When I am afraid, I will trust in you.' Trust doesn't come easy for you, Rita. I know that. But you can believe in this. You can trust God."

Rita lifted her head, remaining silent. Her dark eyes looked up into Mark's. She basked in the hope that Mark's encouragement would prove true. Trust was not an easy thing for Rita Eriksson. But, trust in God was a start, and Rita was eager to take that first wobbly step forward.

Chapter 13

The next day dawned bright and clear with frosty, cold temperatures that left a filigree of ice upon the tent walls. Rita found herself no worse for her experience and began the day by going outside and joining Mark in a hesitant prayer. After that, when the silence threatened to unnerve her, Rita fell back to her defensive nature.

"Shouldn't we be pushing on for Iditarod?" she questioned as she began to repack her sled.

"Definitely. We've lost a lot of time, and since the weather has cleared, the others will no doubt have already passed us," Mark replied, acting as though it wasn't a big deal.

Rita's face fell. "I wanted to be the first to Iditarod. I wanted to give Dad the ingots."

"They wouldn't mean much to him,"

Mark replied. "He'd rather know that you enjoyed yourself and that you managed to stay alive and well."

"How would you know?" Rita retorted. "I know it meant a great deal to Dad to have won those ingots."

"Then you really don't know him very well at all," Mark spoke behind steamy breath.

"What's that supposed to mean? He is *my* father," Rita said.

"The money, prizes, and laurels were never what drove your father to race the Iditarod," Mark began. "As a young man he traveled these trails in order to deliver the mail. He raced because he needed to prove to himself that he could do it one last time. He needed to taste the ice with each breath, to hear the silence of the interior, and feel the dogs working beneath his hands. The ingots never meant to him what they obviously mean to you."

Rita felt a rage building inside her. How dare Mark tell her what her father felt or who he was. She opened her mouth to speak and then shut it again. What could she say that would make any sense? It wasn't easy to refute the truth. Mark was right, and that's what bothered her most. She walked away to consider his words, still feeling his eyes burning holes through her façade.

Retracing their way back to the trail proved easier than either one had imagined. Rita was surprised to learn that she'd been only a matter of miles from Iditarod. Somehow, through the blizzard and all of the trials that had plagued her way, Rita had still managed to keep the team going in the right direction.

"That's some nose," Mark teased as they made their way to the checkpoint officials. "You wandered around, blind in a snowstorm for three days, and still managed to put yourself in a decent position to regain the lost time."

Rita said nothing as people pressed in around her.

"We'd just about given up hope of finding you," one man remarked behind a fur-trimmed parka. "Are you injured?"

"No," Rita answered. "A little frostbite on my face, but nothing serious."

"I guess that's pretty typical," the man laughed. "I've heard more than one racer talk about his or her new Iditarod skin. Losing frostbitten skin off your face is pretty routine, and the skin beneath is baby soft."

Rita smiled and waited for the officials to check her dogs over. She'd lost track of Mark, and it wasn't until she overheard a comment by the man who'd first spoken to her that Rita realized something was wrong.

"I'm sorry," she said, placing a hand on the man's parka, "I couldn't help overhear your comment that Mark Williams is in some kind of trouble."

The man turned and pushed back his parka enough to reveal a weather-lined face with a graying beard. "He disqualified himself coming out after you. He disobeyed the official's direct order to stay in Ophir after a freeze was put on the race."

"But he only left to come after me. What about the Good Samaritan Rule? It wasn't that he was trying to get ahead in the race. No doubt there are plenty of racers who've moved out ahead of us. Mark isn't a threat to anyone's victory," Rita protested.

"I'm just working here," the man said and threw up his hands. "But as I understand it, the problem isn't that he helped you so much as he disregarded a direct order. The real decision has to come from a three-member panel of the race officials. They're appointed by the Iditarod Race

Marshall and they have to reach a unanimous decision."

"Then I need to get word to them," Rita said, suddenly fearing that Mark would have come all this way, only to be disqualified by an unselfish act of concern for her.

"I'm not sure what to tell you," the man replied. "You'd probably better talk to the man in charge. He's over there in the blue coveralls."

"Thank you." Rita saw to her dogs, then went in search of the race official.

Although Rita had fully intended to push right out of Iditarod and head for Shageluk on the Innoko River, she found herself unable to continue until she learned of Mark's fate.

She'd explained everything she could to the official and pleaded Mark's case in every way she could conceive. The man had been sympathetic and considerate of her testimony and promised that the officials would take everything into consideration. The answer would be radioed to them within a matter of minutes.

"I'm sorry for the trouble I've caused you, Mark." Rita's sincerity was evident as she took a seat beside her father's partner.

"I would do it all again," Mark said in a

peaceful way that eluded Rita.

"Aren't you angry?"

"No," Mark said with a shake of his head. "Why should I be?" He looked up from where he'd been mending a harness. Mark was never one for wasting a single minute. "Anger wouldn't change a thing and would only ruin this beautiful day."

"I've possibly cost you the race. They may not let you finish the Iditarod. Doesn't that mean anything? After all, that's why we're here," Rita argued.

"I would debate that," Mark said matter-of-factly. "God has many purposes for us in life. I believe it's entirely possible that the only reason I raced this year was in order to be there for you. God knew you'd need help, both physically and spiritually. If He used me for that purpose, then I'm content."

"You mean to tell me," Rita began, "that you wouldn't be the least bit disappointed if they disqualified you here and now?"

"Of course I'd be disappointed," Mark replied. "I planned for this race all year, just like you did. I'm just saying that the race isn't everything. I made the decision, knowing full well what the possible consequences could be. You nearly lost your life out there, Rita. Is life so unimportant to you that you wouldn't risk being disqualified from the Iditarod if it meant that you could save someone from dying?"

Rita swallowed hard. She'd always put herself first, and now she couldn't honestly say whether she would have given up her lead, even the race, to help someone else out of their own foolishness. Suddenly, Rita felt repulsed at the image she had of herself. Would she really have let someone die?

Mark sensed the inner struggle in Rita. His sympathy for her was evident. "You've had a hard time of it, Rita. Nevertheless, I don't doubt for one minute that you would not only risk disqualification of the race, but that you'd risk your very life in order to save another. You aren't the vicious, heartless person you believe yourself to be."

"I don't know about that," Rita admitted. "You may know my father well, but you don't know me."

Mark smiled in a way that caused Rita's heart to race. "I think I know you better than you imagine."

"Just because you rescued me doesn't mean you know everything about me." Rita's words were strangely soft-spoken.

"I wouldn't pretend to know everything about you, Miss Eriksson," Mark said with a chuckle. "I just propose to have more insight than you give me credit for."

"Williams!" the race official's voice rang out. He crossed the distance with long, quick strides. "The panel has cleared you to continue. You haven't been disqualified!"

The small crowd that had waited to hear the announcement gave up a cheer, while Mark and Rita embraced without thinking.

"I'm so glad!" Rita nearly squealed. Mark wrapped his arms around her, lifting her into the air and twirling her around.

"Me, too!" he replied then placed a kiss firmly upon Rita's lips.

Rita found herself returning Mark's kiss before her mind could offer up any protest. She lingered in his arms while the people around them offered congratulatory praises and encouraging words. When the revelry died down, Rita's senses seemed to return. She became very aware of Mark's firm hold and dropped her arms.

Raising her eyes slowly, she found Mark's laughing eyes and smug expression. "I told you I knew you better than you think."

Rita felt her face turn hot in spite of the subzero temperatures. She pushed away from Mark, stammering for something to say, but words escaped her.

"You'd best get a move on it," someone said, and Rita nodded.

"Yes, I'm going," she said and backed away from Mark. He was still standing there, looking quite satisfied with himself, when Rita finished securing her team.

Moving out of Iditarod, Rita's mind moved in a hundred different directions. She'd become a Christian, but what did that really mean in the way that she'd now live her life? Could she somehow find a way to reach out to her mother and overcome the past?

She smiled to herself as she imagined her father's pleasure in her decision to accept Christ. He could rest easy now, and that gave Rita peace. Maybe it wasn't too late to make up for the past.

She tried to ignore the images of Mark in her mind, but when his voice called out behind her in the traditional "Trail!" requesting that she yield the right-of-way to his passing team, Rita couldn't help but think of him.

She glanced up behind dark glasses as Mark gave her a brief salute and was gone. Watching his team disappear in the distance, Rita found that she had no desire to pursue him. She needed distance between them. Distance to think and to understand why she'd so shamelessly reacted to Mark's kiss.

After eight days on the Iditarod, the Yukon River presented itself to Rita. She was tired of the ice, cold, and wind, but that was what this race was all about — that and inner strength, guts and sheer willpower.

Now over six hundred fifty miles from the starting line of the race with a little over five hundred yet to go, sleep was quickly becoming a thing of the past.

Rita found the breaks shorter in length and farther apart. She craved sleep like a starving man craved food. Pushing north on the frozen river, Rita found it necessary to strap herself to the sled to prevent falling off of it when she dozed. She struggled to stay awake, hearing voices that weren't there, seeing sights that had never known creation in the real world.

She made her checkpoints at Grayling, Eagle Island, and finally Kaltag before moving west toward the Bering Sea and Unalakleet. Following trails that were centuries old, Rita pressed her team along the Kaltag Portage for nearly one hundred miles. The routine of fighting fierce winds and death-defying cold with brief naps and feeding periods took an even greater toll. Rita was nearing exhaustion and wouldn't feel free to sleep for any long period of time until she reached White Mountain, where she'd have to take a mandatory six-hour stopover. Until then, she'd have to catch just bits and pieces of rest on the way.

Unalakleet, "place where the east wind blows," was an Inupiat Eskimo village of nearly eight hundred people. Positioned on the Bering Sea, this small town represented the place where camaraderie gave way to competition. It was here that racers would dump off all but their most necessary equipment and often pick up sleek, lightweight racing sleds for the final push into Nome.

After a welcome of sirens and bells from the town's natives, Rita fed the dogs and left them to rest while she changed over her sled and made decisions about her supplies. Every time a new team came into sight, the revelry would sound again, reminding Rita of her competition. In all the time since she'd last seen Mark, Rita hadn't even thought to check on his progress. Now Rita's only competition was herself. It wasn't that she didn't want to win the race, it was just that everything had changed on the way to Iditarod. Now, it was enough to push herself to the limit and do her best without causing harm to the team or risking them in any way.

Each team was appointed to a Unalakleet family and cared for during their stopover. Rita was grateful for her host family and made her way to an offered meal and bed, after finishing with her sled. It was a tradition Rita totally approved of and found herself thanking God for as she set her alarm and fell instantly into deep sleep.

Hours later, Rita awoke to a rosy dawn and steaming coffee. She ate and chatted with her host before seeing to her duties. With the final stretches of the race ahead of her, Rita would do as most of the other team drivers did and reduce the number of dogs on her team. She had mentally calculated each choice after watching her dogs on the trail.

She walked quickly among the dogs, surveying and deciding before finally reducing the team to ten. The other dogs were then taken to the holding pens to be flown back to Anchorage. It was hard to part with any of them, and Rita felt almost as though she were betraying them, even knowing that it was for their benefit.

Reluctantly, Rita departed Unalakleet following two other teams as the trail rose into the coastal Blueberry Hills. Their next checkpoint would be Shaktoolik.

Rita found herself surprisingly invigorated after her rest in Unalakleet. Maybe it was changing the sled and dropping the dogs, but whatever it was, Rita suddenly found herself revitalized and eager to race.

She pushed out against the twenty-mile-an-hour gusts that bore down from the northwest to pass two teams. With each gained position she felt the race spirit alive and well within her heart. She wanted to do well and make her father proud!

Shaktoolik was only forty miles from Unalakleet, and the time passed so quickly that Rita could scarcely believe her good fortune. She had gained a total of three positions and learned that another four teams ahead of her were still resting at the checkpoint. Deciding to push on, Rita's enthusiasm was picked up by the dogs, who yipped and strained to be down the trail at a run.

Land soon gave way to frozen Norton Bay. This was the part of the race that Rita had feared most. It unnerved her to realize, as her team moved out across the ice, that beneath her was nothing but water. Sure, there was a thick frozen surface, but an early warming or sudden storm could quickly create a life-and-death situation.

The skies were still clear, however, and in spite of the strong winds, Rita found the trail markers easily. She settled her nerves by reminding herself that all was in God's hands and pulled her parka hood tight against the wind.

She stopped once on the icy surface to change booties on her dogs and offer them a quick snack of honeyballs. Her fingers numbed as she whipped off her gloves and mittens to pull off worn, tattered booties and replace them with new ones.

Soon they were back on their way and Rita looked forward to the next checkpoint. For the first time she found herself wanting to know what Mark's ranking was and how he was doing. With a fondness that startled her, she remembered his embrace. She wanted to let go of her fears and reach out to Mark, but should she?

"What should I do, God?" Rita found herself praying. "For so many years I've put people away from me. I've fought to keep my distance and never let people too close. I can't ignore how Mark made me feel, Lord, but what do I do?"

Conditions started to deteriorate as Rita's team approached the checkpoint at Kouk on the opposite shore of Norton Bay. The winds had picked up to a fierce forty miles per hour with a heavy blizzard to present near-whiteout conditions. Rita pulled into the checkpoint riding on sheer nerves and adrenaline.

"You're doing a fine job, Ms. Eriksson," the official told her. "How are your dogs doing?"

"Great," Rita gasped for air; she had run the last mile to lighten the load for her dogs.

"You've moved into nineteenth place," the man added as he walked away.

"Wait a minute," Rita called out. "What about Mark Williams?"

"Let me see," the man replied and paused to check his list. "He was here eight hours ago."

Rita smiled to herself. "Thanks. Has anyone crossed the finish line yet?"

"Not yet, but it's getting close. Several of the front runners will soon be within reach of it. My guess on a finish time will be thirteen days and some odd hours."

"Fantastic!" Rita exclaimed. She

couldn't imagine the speed that the others would have to maintain to pull off a thirteen-day race completion. Her own pace had been grueling enough.

"Let him do well, Lord," Rita whispered as she went about heating food and water for the dogs. "I want Mark to do well," she added, knowing that she meant it with all her heart.

Chapter 14

Rita crossed the finish line in Nome amidst the cheers of well-wishers and residents. Television cameras still worked to capture the race; the healthy finish of Rita in seventeenth place merited special attention. It would also earn her the sum of six thousand dollars. Rita found herself calculating expenses for the race; they might just break even.

Rita answered questions for the press, giving them her outlook and feel for the final miles of the trail. They also quizzed her about her lost days near Iditarod, and Rita was quick to give Mark credit for her rescue.

"I probably wouldn't be here now if it weren't for Mark Williams," Rita told a newspaper reporter. "He risked not only disqualification from the race, but his life in order to go out and search for me."

"Mark Williams is your father's partner in the Eriksson Dog Kennel, is he not?" the man questioned her.

"That's true," Rita admitted. "He's also a good friend of the family."

"Any chance that you and he are more than good friends?" the man asked with a grin.

Rita was surprised at the question and noticed that the other reporters awaited her answer with an almost anxious look.

"I'd say that's between Rita and me," Mark's voice rang out from somewhere behind the crowd. "Now, if you don't mind, we need to care for the dogs." Then in a whisper for only Rita's ears, Mark added, "Good to see you, Texas Rita."

There was a bustle of activity and several other questions posed, but Mark waved them off and managed to pull Rita away from the press.

"Why did you bait them like that?" Rita asked, forgetting how happy she was to see him.

Mark laughed. "I thought it sounded good." Mark thrust his gloved hands deep into his pockets and shrugged his shoulders. Rita thought he looked rather like a little boy who'd been caught red-handed with the cookie jar.

"But you saw the way they reacted to your reply. You might as well have told them something far-fetched, like we were planning our wedding," retorted Rita.

Mark grinned and reached out to take hold of her arm. "And what would be so bad about that?"

Rita stared up in shocked surprise. She opened her mouth to answer but never got the chance, for just then her aunt Julie appeared in the path before them.

"Aunt Julie!" Rita cried and fell into the older woman's arms. "I'm so glad you're here. I wasn't sure I'd make it, but I knew you'd be waiting here for me and that helped me to push on."

"I knew you could do it," Julie remarked beneath layers of mufflers and fur. "You've got that tenacious Swedish blood from your grandfather Eriksson. You put your mind to complete the race and the rest just followed naturally."

Rita laughed at her aunt's words. She turned to say something to Mark, only to realize he'd slipped away from her. She looked around her, hoping to catch a glimpse of him, but to no avail. People filled in every inch of the street and the noise was incredible.

"Are you looking for that young man of

yours?" Julie questioned loudly.

Rita put her hands on her hips and with a raised eyebrow asked, "Why do you call him 'that young man of yours?' "

Julie smiled. "Never mind. We can talk about it at home. I've got a bed ready and waiting."

"A real bed?" Rita teasingly questioned. She looked among the crowd for her uncle Sam before turning back to Julie. "Where's Uncle Sam? I can't imagine that he'd miss the race. He isn't sick, is he?"

Julie patted Rita's arm. "You worry too much. I said we'd catch everything up at home. Come on." Julie motioned to Rita, but she held back.

"Really, it sounds great," Rita sighed, "but first —"

"First come the dogs," Julie interrupted and laughed. "They always come first," she added, linking her arm with Rita's. "Oh, by the way," Julie said with a wink, "Mark came in fifth."

Rita's dogs were taken in crates to the airport, but not before she gave each one a heartfelt thank you. Dandy seemed to sense that he'd done quite well and jumped up and down in his harness until Rita finally calmed him down. She stood watching the transport truck disappear down the road when she felt familiar hands on her shoulders.

"Hi, Seventeen," Mark's deep voice called out in the silence.

Rita turned quickly. At least calling her Seventeen wouldn't require an explanation. "Mark! I wondered where you went. Thanks for the help with the dogs. I still can't believe I really finished the race."

"No problem," Mark replied, acting as though their earlier conversation had never taken place. "I did want to point out, however, that you weren't there to greet me as I crossed the finish line." His teasing nature was infectious.

Rita couldn't help but grin. "I know, Number Five. I guess next year I'll just have to rectify that problem."

"Next year?" Mark questioned with a chuckle. "What makes you think I'll let you come next year?"

"What makes you presume that you'll have any say?" Rita's determined look made Mark back down with a laugh.

"I guess we can discuss it later," he added.

"Everyone keeps saying that," Rita replied and picked up the bag of things she'd decided to keep with her rather than ship back home. "I'm staying with my aunt, Julie Curtiss. I'm sure you'd be welcome to drop over."

"Maybe I will," Mark answered. "We'll see."

Rita followed her aunt Julie up the long shoveled walkway, grateful that she'd finally be able to take a hot shower and sleep in a real bed.

Julie unlocked the door of her two-storied house and ushered her niece inside; the pungent aroma of flowers filled the air.

"Umm," Rita said, putting her bag down on the entryway floor. "It smells like a florist shop in here."

"It should," Julie replied and led Rita to the living room, where flowers and potted plants graced every tabletop.

"They're beautiful!" Rita exclaimed. "Where did they all come from?"

"Sam's funeral," Julie said softly. "He died the day you started the Iditarod."

Rita dropped quietly into a nearby chair. "Dead? Uncle Sam is dead?"

Julie pulled off her heavy coat and cast it aside. "Yes. I know it's hard to believe. I wish there could have been an easier way to tell you." Julie couldn't help but sympathize with the great shock her niece had

201

just been dealt. August hadn't handled it any better when Julie had telephoned him with the news.

"It's hard for me to accept because it feels as though he's right here. His things are still here. His guitar still sits in its case against the wall. His reading glasses are still on the table over there," Julie said and pointed.

"Wha . . . what happened?" Rita asked as tears spilled down her cheeks.

"He died in his sleep, Rita." Julie smiled. "We'd had a wonderful evening with friends and had come home to discuss you and the race. Sam bet you'd place in the top twenty and, sure enough, here you are. Then we climbed into bed, talked some more, and held each other close. When I woke up in the morning, he was gone."

"You talk about it so calmly," Rita sobbed. "I don't know how you bear it."

"Sam's not all that far away," Julie answered. "He's not gone forever . . . he's just waiting in heaven."

Rita nodded. "But you're here, Aunt Julie."

Julie smiled and eased back against the chair. "Yes, that is the hard part. I must wait and join him later. But you know, a long time ago, when I traveled the old village trails as a public health nurse, Sam often had to wait for me here at home.

"I remember how hard the separation was and how eagerly I would hurry home to be with him again. Sam always kept a light burning for me in the window . . . it was our way of letting the other one know that we'd not forgotten them." Julie got up and crossed the room. She pulled back heavy drapery to reveal a small lamp. Its soft glowing bulb burned as a bright reminder that Sam was not forgotten.

"I know that Sam's burning one for me in heaven," Julie said, with a single tear touching her wrinkled cheek. "I'll make my way home when the time is right."

Rita rushed to her aunt and held her. "Oh, Aunt Julie, I'm so sorry he's gone. I loved him a great deal. He always made me laugh." Her voice broke into sobs. "I'm sorry that I'm not offering you comfort . . . blubbering as I am."

"It's all right, Rita. I miss him, too. I didn't say it was easy. But at least I know where he is."

Rita nodded and pulled back and wiped her eyes. "Aunt Julie, I asked Jesus to be my Savior." The sudden revelation seemed fitting.

Julie's face lit up with such joy that Rita

thought she would shout. "I've prayed that you would. Now, you don't have to worry about death. Not Sam's or mine, or even your mom or dad's. You'll see us again in heaven and you don't need to fear life or death."

Rita shook her head. "I want it to be that real to me, Aunt Julie, but . . ."

"But?"

Rita led Julie to the sofa, where both women dropped wearily.

"But, I don't feel anything really different. Oh, I think I feel peace. You know, the kind of peace that you get when you stop fighting something and give in. You're still not sure you understand what you're getting yourself into, but you feel better in just having done something."

Julie laughed. "Oh, Rita, I do understand. Let me assure you, God is very much alive and working in your heart. Your salvation is quite real."

Rita shook her head. "I want to believe that. I said the words and I believed them true. It's just that I don't know what comes next. Doesn't that sound stupid? I mean, here I am, a church kid who spent a lifetime involved in Sunday school and Bible memory contests, but I don't know what to do next or how to find out."

Julie took Rita's hand in her own aged one. "Rita, God loves you. You understand this, don't you?"

"Of course," Rita replied.

"No, I mean," Julie reemphasized the words, "God loves *you,* Rita. God loves Rita Eriksson."

Rita's puzzled look caused Julie to continue. "God knows you better than you know yourself, Rita. He formed you in your mother's womb and molded you into the person you became. He patiently waited for you to turn back to Him and, because He loved you, Rita, He gave you a way back through Jesus. You can count on that way to be real, and even though you can't see the bridge that Jesus' sacrifice gave you, it's there.

"It's that old issue of trust," Julie continued. "God has given many promises in the Bible. You don't have to worry that some are true and others aren't. God didn't allow the Word to be created for some kind of show. It's genuine and real, and it offers you all the guidance and hope that you will ever need. You must have the faith to accept God's gift and live for Him."

Rita nodded slowly. "I guess my faith is very weak."

"No, Rita," Julie said, squeezing Rita's hand. "It's just newborn. It's tiny and small but very much alive and surprisingly strong. Give it time and it will grow as you feed on the Word and rest in the Lord. Now," Julie said as she glanced at the clock on her wall, "catching up on everything else will wait. You need to go to bed. Come along."

Julie showed Rita to her room and gave her a kiss on the cheek before closing the door. Rita shed her coveralls and dropped to her knees. "Oh, God, thank You for Aunt Julie. She's such a strong and wise woman. I want to know You like she does and I want my faith to grow." Rita started to get to her feet but stopped. "And, Lord, please help her not to be lonely without Uncle Sam, Amen."

Chapter 15

The next day Rita answered the door of her aunt Julie's house while her aunt prepared breakfast in the kitchen.

A young man stood holding a white box and clipboard. "I have a delivery for Rita Eriksson," he said as he studied the paper.

"That's me," Rita replied and signed for the delivery. She tipped the delivery man and went back to the warmth of her aunt's kitchen.

"Just what we need," Rita mused, "more flowers."

"Who are they from?" Julie questioned as she loaded the table with more food than she or Rita could possibly finish.

"I don't know," Rita replied and opened the large box. Inside was a stately-looking, white Stetson hat. "Well, what do you know," Rita gasped, staring at the hat.

Julie peered over her shoulder. "We've

better use for that than flowers. Who's it from?"

Rita couldn't speak for a moment. She knew full well who the hat was from, but it would be impossible to explain to Julie. "Here's the card," Rita finally replied. "It says, 'Congratulations, Texas Rita. What's so far-fetched about —' " Rita fell silent as she glanced over the words that followed.

"What's so far-fetched about what?" Julie inquired, joining Rita at the table. "And what's with the Texas Rita stuff?"

Rita shook her head. The gift was from Mark and he wanted to know what was so far-fetched about their planning a wedding. How could Rita explain that to her aunt?

"It's nothing, Julie," she said and put the card in her pocket. "It's from Mark and he's just giving me a hard time because I once mentioned wanting to move to Texas."

"He's a good man, Rita." Julie's words were true and Rita knew it full well.

"I know," she finally murmured and waited for Julie to pray over their food.

Julie sensed Rita's reluctance to discuss the matter any more. Instead, she prayed a short blessing and offered her niece breakfast.

Rita felt relief to see that Julie was willing to drop the matter. Now, if only she could avoid Mark. There was no way she'd be able to face him and discuss anything rationally.

There were several parties and presentations at which Rita would have to be present. Of course, she could always feign being sick, but that would go against her newfound principles. Besides, it would no doubt bring Mark to her side, and in the privacy of her aunt's home, Rita knew it would be more than she could bear.

Rita made plans for her trip back to Anchorage amidst meeting her obligations in finishing the formalities of the race. There was a party she was to attend that would honor all those who'd run the race. Julie had agreed to accompany Rita, but on the night of the party, Julie was sick in bed with a bad cold.

"I'll be just fine, Rita," Julie chided her niece. "You go to the party and have fun. I'm just being cautious with myself, knowing how easily I seem to contract pneumonia."

"But I could stay here and take care of you," Rita said, nearly pleading. She was desperate to stay out of Mark's reach.

"I wouldn't hear of it. You've earned your laurels. I insist you go and party with your friends and have a good time. I'm sure if you called Mark at the hotel, he'd be more than happy to come escort you to the party," Julie added.

"Yes, I'm sure he would be," Rita said and walked to the door. "That's what I'm afraid of."

Julie chuckled and covered it with a cough. Rita knew her aunt was good-naturedly trying to help her to see the good side of Mark's interest. Rita just shook her head, however, and went to get ready for the party.

The evening passed without mishap, and Rita was beginning to have confidence that she just might avoid Mark, when suddenly he was at her side.

"I'd like to have a moment of your time," he whispered in her ear. Taking hold of her hand, he added, "If you aren't too busy."

Rita trembled at his touch and her eyes darkened to ebony.

Against her will, she looked up and saw the determination in Mark's face.

"All right." She barely got the words out before Mark was leading her down the corridor to the coat-check room.

"Let's walk," he suggested and called for their coats.

Rita felt her stomach turn flip-flops when Mark helped her on with her coat. She heard an inner voice that told her to run back to the safety of her aunt's house, but her legs refused to move.

"Are you ready?" Mark questioned, seeing that Rita was rooted in place. "You ought to have a good hat," he added with a grin.

It pulled Rita from her stupor. "I have one," she said with a smirk, "but my boots don't match."

Mark laughed heartily. "We'll have to rectify that."

Outside, the town was still overrun with visitors and extended race parties. Mark led Rita down a quiet side street and off to a more secluded part of town. Rita sensed Mark growing more serious.

"I've wanted to talk to you for days, but you were avoiding me," Mark began. "I figured out if I didn't force my hand I'd have to wait until we got back to your folks' house, and I didn't want to wait."

Rita didn't even look up. She shuffled along at Mark's side waiting for the rest of his speech.

"I don't know why you are having trouble facing me, Rita." Mark's words weren't what Rita had expected.

Her head snapped up and the independent spirit in her won over. "I'm not having trouble facing you," she lied.

"You sure you want to stay with that story, ma'am?" Mark questioned, sounding every bit the law official.

"No, I . . . well . . . ," Rita stammered. "So I was avoiding you. What of it?"

Mark laughed out loud and pulled Rita with him. "Come on, let's have some coffee. I know a quiet little place."

Rita soon found herself seated with Mark as the only guests of the small café. Mark ordered them coffee and continued his conversation as though nothing had caused any break in his thought.

"Why are you avoiding me, Rita?"

"I don't know," she managed to answer. Her cheeks were flushed and her stomach churned. Why couldn't he just drop the subject and talk about something else?

"I think you do know," Mark pressed. "I think you know how I feel about you and I think you feel the same way."

"I don't know what you're talking about," Rita replied, and turned her attention to the coffee that the waitress had just brought.

"I've come to care a great deal about you, Rita. At first, I thought it was just because of my loyalty to August, but that passed real quick," he said with a grin. "I love you, Rita."

The words were bold and without hesitation, no teasing and not a hint of sarcasm. Rita nearly spit out her coffee at the declaration. Her eyes opened wide and her mouth dropped open. How could he say something so important with no more warning than that?

"You what?" She thought she'd only questioned Mark in her mind, but the words vocalized themselves aloud.

"You heard me," Mark replied patiently. "I love you. Furthermore, I want you to be my wife. I want us to get married right away, even before we go back home."

"I don't believe this," Rita gasped. "I can't believe that you're saying any of this."

"Would you like me to get down on one knee?" he teased.

"I'm serious," Rita said in an offended tone. "How can you joke at a time like this?"

"I'm serious," Mark said, moving from the chair to put one knee on the floor.

"Get up," Rita said between clenched

teeth. "Get up before somebody sees you."

"I won't get up until you say that you'll marry me," Mark restated.

Rita wanted to run, but instead tears came to her eyes, and before she could control them, she was nearly hysterical. Mark got up and quickly offered her his handkerchief.

"I'm sorry, Rita," he said softly. He sat back down and waited for Rita to regain control of her emotions.

"No," Rita whispered. "I'm the one who's sorry. You're a good man and I can't imagine why you would continue to care about me after all that's taken place between us."

"The past is gone," Mark offered. "I don't hold anything against you and I hope you don't hold anything against me."

"I don't," Rita said, shaking her head. "I just can't deal with all of this right now. I don't know what I feel or think. I was just trying to understand Christianity and where I stood with God and now this. I can't do it, Mark. I can't deal with you and God at the same time."

"But you've resolved your relationship with God. I was there, remember? I know that you've got a lot of questions, but they'll all get answers in time." Mark paused for a moment, still feeling disbelief for Rita's display of emotions. "I know you care about me. No, I'm certain you love me," Mark proclaimed.

Rita dried her eyes and held back the torrent of new tears that threatened to flow. "I'm glad you're certain, because I don't know what I feel."

They sat in silence for several minutes before Mark surprised them both and got to his feet. "I do love you, Rita. There will always be a place for you back home. I'll be there and you'll know where to find me. Just remember this," he added with a gentle smile, "I'm not the kind of man who gives up. I'm very patient and I can wait you out. Some day you'll come to me and I'll be there with open arms just for you, Texas Rita."

He threw some money down on the table and walked from the café, still carrying his coat. Rita stared after him in wonderment. He wasn't mad or, if he was, he held it in so that not a single trace made itself known to Rita.

She marveled at his confidence and peace. "How could he be so certain of his feelings?" she whispered. Yet, even as she questioned his actions, Rita knew in her heart that he was right. She did care for him. She did love him. But how was she supposed to deal with those feelings?

Rita left the café and took the long way back to her aunt's house. She had to think things through and, in spite of the cold, Rita took her time pondering the situation.

"Aunt Julie was right," Rita muttered aloud. "I'm afraid to trust Mark, just like I was afraid to trust God." She fell silent and wondered if perhaps she was still afraid to trust God.

"It's all so new to me, God," she whispered to the night air. "I know that I'm supposed to have faith and to trust, but You know that doesn't come easy for me. Now, Mark is asking for the same thing. He wants to marry me, Lord. What am I supposed to do?"

She approached the Curtiss house and caught sight of the light in the window — Sam's light, Julie's light. The reminder of a love that had lasted through childbirth, death, wars, and all that came from the process of living.

Rita thought of the way Sam would look at Julie. There had always been so much love in his eyes, and Rita had marveled at it even as a teenager. How could anyone ever share a love like that and make it last a lifetime?

Rita looked up to the skies as if hoping that some celestial answer would be written across the heavens. Could it be possible that Mark loved her in the same way that Sam had loved Julie? Was it possible that Rita was throwing away her only chance for that kind of love?

She made her way quickly into the house and nearly ran up the stairs to get to her aunt's room. A light from beneath the door gave Rita all the prompting she needed.

She knocked lightly and called, "Aunt Julie, are you still awake?"

"Come on in, Rita," Julie answered. "What's going on?"

Rita left her coat in the hall and crossed the room to her aunt's bed. "I need to talk."

Julie smiled and patted the bed. "Have a seat and tell me what's on your mind."

Rita lost no time. "Mark asked me to marry him."

Julie clapped her hands together. "How wonderful!"

Rita frowned. "I told him no."

"You did what?" Julie questioned.

"I told him no. Oh, Aunt Julie, I can't marry Mark. I don't know how I feel about him. One minute I think I love him, the next minute I don't think I even know the meaning of the word." Rita threw up her hands. "How can I promise to love and cherish someone, when I'm not even sure what it means to love."

"But, Rita," said Julie, "you've known what it is to be loved and to love. You've had your family and friends —"

"No," Rita interrupted. "I never felt loved by any of my friends. I always kept them at arm's length. It was my fault, but, Aunt Julie, I never let any of them get close enough to love them or for them to love me."

"But your family," Julie protested, "they love you and surely you love them. You love me, don't you?"

"Of course," Rita replied. It hurt so much to think her aunt might question her love. "You've always been there for me. You've always loved me."

"Well then, what is it?" Julie continued. "Your mother and father love you. Your brothers and sisters love you. How can you say you don't know how to love or be loved?"

Rita hung her head. "I hardly know my brothers and sisters."

"Whose fault is that?" Julie questioned sternly.

"I know it's partially my fault," Rita admitted. "But some of it is their fault."

"You can't deal with other than what you, yourself, control. Your anger and alienation toward them is where you must begin. Let go of the past and the distances that separated you. When you get home, why not write each of them a long letter. Tell them how you feel. I think you'd be surprised at their response," Julie suggested.

"What about Mother?" Rita finally braved the question.

"What about her?"

"She never wanted me, Aunt Julie. I heard her say it. She can't love me if she didn't even want me." Rita broke down.

"Talk to her, Rita. Talk to her and let her explain. I know Beth loves you and I know it hurts her when she believes, by your actions, that you don't love her," Julie said, holding her arms open to Rita's sobbing form.

Rita fell into her aunt's embrace like a small, hurt child. "I want her to love me, Aunt Julie. I want my mother to love me."

"Child, she already does. Give her a chance to show you," Julie said in a calming way. "Give them all a chance, Rita. Your mother, God, Mark . . . let them show you how important you are to them. Let them love you."

Chapter 16

Anchorage looked almost foreign to Rita. She realized how little attention she'd paid the town before the race. After living there for five years, she'd taken it for granted. Now, looking out from her hotel window, Rita found herself wishing she could be back in Tok.

For over an hour she watched as the townspeople hustled to beat the clock. Traffic moved at a quick clip along the busy, inner-city streets, while pedestrians fought competitively for their right to cross intersections.

Store windows sported huge signs that called the public inside to late winter sales and discounted prices. It was all so busy, so noisy, and completely out of sync with what Rita had just been doing for the last year.

Rita was surprised to find that she

missed the quiet of her woods and the vast openness of rural life. She missed the dogs and the roar of the wind through the trees. Even the northern lights would be difficult to see through the harsh city lights. Rita longed for home.

"What am I going to do now?" she whispered to the city. "I don't belong here and I want to go home. But should I go back?"

And what of Mark? her heart questioned. He loved her and she knew she loved him. Dare she give up her independence and tear down the walls that separated them? Dare she return his love as openly as he gave his?

A knock at the door brought Rita back to reality. She crossed the room, opened the door, and found her parents on the other side.

"Mom! Dad!" squealed Rita. She embraced them both at once and missed the look of surprise they shared over her shoulder. "I wondered when you were going to get here. How are you? How are the dogs?"

"Fine to both questions," August said with a laugh. "If I didn't know better, I'd say you missed us."

"What makes you think you know better?" Rita questioned. "I did miss you and I'm very glad to see you here. In fact, I have something important to tell you both."

August and Beth steadied each other. With Rita it was hard to tell what she might have in mind. Over the years they'd learned to take her declarations in stride and knew better than to try and anticipate what their daughter might say.

"Come and sit down," Rita said, taking them to a small table. "There are only two chairs, so I'll sit on the bed."

Her parents nodded and moved almost apprehensively to the chairs. Rita swallowed hard and tried to think of just the right words.

"I did a lot of thinking out on the trail," she began. "I know the reports of my foolishness have already reached the papers and television, so I realize how worried you must have been. I want to apologize for not calling you, but I had to think through a great deal."

August and Beth hung on their daughter's every word. They had worried about her. Worried that her stubborn pride would claim her life and remembered having to sit by and wait until news of their youngest confirmed that she was safe.

Rita paused for a moment. She still had

a touch of pride that worried about her mother's reaction to her declaration of faith. If Beth reacted smugly, Rita just knew she'd run from the room. Steadying her nerves, Rita continued.

"Mark found me when I'd just about given up hope of going on. I'd lost the team and things looked pretty bad. I'd managed to make a windbreak by packing snow, but I knew I couldn't last long without my gear and the dogs. Then Mark showed up and everything turned around. That night we talked a lot and I came to be sorry for the problems my stubbornness and independence have caused."

"What are you trying to say, Rita?" August asked.

Rita drew a deep breath. "I guess I'm trying to apologize for the way I've acted in the past. I gave up my pride and accepted Christ as my Savior." She waited and watched Beth for the reaction she feared, but the only thing she saw were the tears in her mother's eyes.

August nodded. "That must have been the hardest decision you've ever made."

Rita was amazed at the peace that settled over the room. She had been so sure of how her parents would respond that she'd literally spent hours deciding how she, herself, would react.

"It was," Rita finally replied.

Beth wiped away the tears in her eyes but remained silent. Rita thought there was a gentler look to her mother. Was it Rita's decision to accept Christ that made her so? Or was Rita just truly seeing her mother for the first time?

A knock sounded at the door and Rita hesitantly answered it. There was still much more she wanted to say, especially to her mother. She didn't like the idea of an interruption.

"Yes?" she questioned the hotel employee who waited on the other side.

"Is Mr. Eriksson here?"

"Yes, I'm August Eriksson," August said, coming to stand beside Rita.

"There's a gentleman in the lobby who wishes to speak to you. I believe he's a reporter," the man responded.

August shrugged his shoulders. "Don't know what he'd want to talk to me about, but let's go. I'll be right back."

Rita felt almost relieved that her father had something else to do. She had really wanted to talk to her mother in private. Closing the door behind her father, Rita went back to the table.

"I'm glad we'll have a few minutes

alone," Rita said, as she took the seat vacated by her father.

"You are?" Beth questioned in surprise.

Rita nodded. "I wanted to ask you to forgive the way I've treated you all these years. I know I was wrong and only acting on hurt and bitter feelings. It was wrong and, despite the fact that you never really wanted me, it wasn't fair to punish you the way I did."

Beth looked as though the wind had been knocked from her. She sat with an expression of complete shock on her face. "What makes you say that I never wanted you?"

Rita felt the tears well in her eyes. "I overheard you. You told my sister that I was such a difficult child to get close to and figured it was your punishment. I heard you say that you never expected to have another child and, in fact, never wanted another child."

Silence hung between the two women as Beth tried to rein in her emotions. "It's true I never planned to have another child after your brother, Edgar. He was, after all, nine years old when you were born." Tears streamed down Beth's face. "I wish I could explain those words. No, I wish I could take them back," Beth whispered.

Rita ached at the sight of her mother's brokenness. In the past, she'd thought on more than one occasion of throwing her mother's words in her face. Somehow, Rita thought it would offer satisfaction or compensation for the pain her mother had caused. Now, it just offered Rita grief and sorrow.

Rita started to speak, but Beth waved her off. "Please, let me finish," she said. "I need to tell you all of it."

Rita nodded and sat back, waiting for her mother to speak.

"I planned to finally spend time with your father," Beth began. "I hoped to dogsled with him or to at least have more time to just be alone with him. We'd never known a time in our marriage when there weren't children and, after twenty-some years of marriage, I intended to get to know him better as a man and husband, rather than a father.

"I found out I was pregnant after thinking that I was going through the change. Mind you, I was happy to be going through the change. My days of having babies were through as far as I was concerned. So, just when I had resigned myself to move into another stage of womanhood, I found that nothing had changed

226

at all. I was pregnant after a nine-year break and it was devastating."

Rita tried to hide the hurt she felt, but she couldn't. Her eyes betrayed her misery, and Beth suddenly realized why all those years had been lost between mother and daughter.

"The story doesn't stop there, however," Beth continued. "I hadn't realized how much I'd distanced myself from you until one day your oldest sister was remarking on the crescent-shaped birthmark you had on your upper thigh. It was like a slap in the face. You were a year old and I didn't even realize you had a birthmark. Suddenly, I started to understand that I'd pretty much given you over to your sisters. They saw you as a chore and not a new baby to play with. They fed you, made clothes for you, changed you, and I surrounded myself in the pretense that I was busy with one project or another and that the experience was good for them.

"Little by little you worked your way into my heart," Beth said with a sad smile. "I found myself watching you. You were such a good baby. So quiet and content. I never had to listen to you fuss and you were never sick. By the time you were a toddler and then old enough for school, I'd come to love you quite dearly. But, the damage, of course, was done. You and I hardly knew each other. For the rest of your life, try as I might, I could never say the right thing or do enough to make it up to you. You never gave me an inch, and I can't really blame you. I didn't deserve an inch." Beth fell silent, trying to determine just how she would say what needed to be said.

Rita cried openly and remembered the lonely little girl who longed for a mother's comfort and instead found disinterested siblings at her side.

"I am so sorry, Rita," Beth sobbed. "I don't deserve for you to forgive me, but I love you so much and I can only beg for you to give me the mercy that I didn't show you."

Rita moved her chair back and stood up. Holding her arms out, she whimpered like a tiny, hurt child, "Momma, I love you!"

Beth threw herself into the arms of her child. The years of pain were cast aside as if they were old, useless coats in springtime warmth. The two women cried long and hard in each other's embrace. Fearful of letting go. Not wanting the moment to pass.

When their tears subsided, Rita was the first to speak.

"I could never understand what I'd done so wrong that no one loved me or wanted me around. I used to lie in bed and one minute I would think of horrible, awful things that I wanted to happen so that I would have my revenge. And the next minute, I'd push it all aside, knowing that I'd gladly give anything I owned to feel loved by you."

"How you must have suffered," Beth whispered. "I can never take that back. I can never make it up to you."

"You don't have to," Rita said, feeling the weight of her misery lifted. "I know now that if I forgive you, then I must let go of the past. That little girl is grown now and we have a future together. Dad told me that his only real worry about leaving this world was that you and I would be alone. Now we can be there for each other. We can start all over."

Beth took hold of her daughter's hands. "I'd like that, Rita. I'd like a chance to put the ugliness aside and start fresh."

"Then that's what we'll do," Rita said and embraced her mother again.

Neither of the women heard August when he returned. When they pulled away laughing, he was there by the door with tears in his eyes.

"Daddy!" Rita exclaimed and held her arms open to him.

August crossed the room, hugging both Beth and Rita to him. "Dare I hope that this means you two have put aside the past?"

"Better than that," Beth replied. "We finally understand the past between us and we're going to forgive it and forget it. Aren't we, Rita?" She looked into her daughter's dark eyes. Eyes so much like her father's that Beth never failed to see August when she saw Rita.

Rita smiled. "We sure are. We have a lot of lost time to make up for."

"Does that mean you'll move back home?" August asked.

"I don't know. I want to get on with my nursing career, but I've come to realize after being home this last year that I don't belong here in Anchorage. I think I'd like to settle down in Tok for a while. Of course, it will all depend on finding a job."

"I'm sure you could work for one of the local doctors," August suggested. "We'd love to have you back home, and that way you and your mom could spend more time together."

"Mom isn't my only concern," Rita said gravely.

"What is it, Rita?" Beth asked in a worried tone.

Rita pulled away from her parents and went back to the table where she slumped into the chair. "It's Mark."

"What about him?" her parents asked in unison.

"I don't know where to begin," Rita said honestly.

August sat on the bed, while Beth joined her daughter at the table. "Just tell us what's wrong," August said.

"I'd love to," Rita admitted. "But I'm not exactly sure what really is wrong."

"Is Mark the reason you don't want to move home?" Beth questioned.

"Yes and no," Rita replied. "Mark told me he loved me and asked me to marry him."

Beth and August exchanged a smile. They thought Mark would make a fine choice for their daughter and didn't hide their obvious pleasure.

"How do you feel about Mark?" Beth asked.

"That's my real dilemma. I know I love him. I just don't know that I'm ready to get married. Allowing people to get close to me is something I'm not very good at. I'm not sure I could do justice to Mark's love." Rita's voice was shaky as she continued. "I guess I'm afraid."

Beth reached out and patted Rita's hand. "Committing yourself in marriage is something you should be very sure of. I will tell you this much, however. Most everyone is afraid of the magnitude of marriage."

"What am I supposed to do then?" Rita questioned. "I mean, I do love him and I don't want to lose him —"

"Why not give Mark credit?" August interjected. "He knows his own heart and he's a good solid thinker. Why not share your apprehension with him and take it one step at a time. I have a feeling Mark will know how to handle the situation."

Rita raised her eyes to her father. "Do you think he will think less of me for my confusion?"

"I don't think it's possible for Mark to think less of you," August answered with a laugh. "He's got it bad for you, Rita. I think if you told him to walk to the moon and back, he'd do it."

"But don't take advantage of him," Beth added. "He's a good man and he deserves to be dealt with in an honest manner. Just talk to him, Rita. If you still have any doubts, work through them and take your time. And Rita," Beth paused, almost fearful of her next suggestion. "Pray about it. Spend a great deal of time in prayer, and I will, too."

Rita nodded. "Of course," she whispered. "I should have thought of that, first thing. Trusting God is something else new to me. I guess I have a lot to learn."

"Don't worry," August said. "God understands all of that and He'll guide you through. Just trust Him for direction, Rita, and when you're afraid, trust Him even more."

Rita couldn't help but smile. "Mark told me about the verse in Psalm Fifty-six that says, 'When I am afraid, I will trust in you.' It seems like a most appropriate verse for me."

Chapter 17

Rita stayed with friends in Anchorage until May. She felt that she needed the time away from everyone in order to sort through her conflicting emotions. She had mailed Mark a brief, but poignant letter that offered no promises but allowed a glimpse of her true feelings for him.

She mostly spent the time in prayer and searching, however. She had determined that it would be foolish to move to Tok without a job. Because of that, Rita gave it over to God and mailed her résumé to all of the area doctors in the small town.

"If God wants me in Tok," Rita had proclaimed, "He will provide me the means to support myself."

When a job offer came at the end of April, Rita was nearly stunned by her answered prayer.

"It was what I prayed for," Rita admitted

to her mother on the telephone. "I guess I'm still so new at this that I didn't really expect an answer."

"Well, I have another answer for you," Beth replied. "Your father has built a small cabin for you about fifteen minutes away. It's closer to Tok than our place, but close enough to home that you could just hike over if you were of a mind to."

Rita shook her head. It seemed fairly obvious that God wanted her in Tok. "That would make it just under thirty minutes into town," she surmised.

"That's true," Beth answered. "If you don't mind, we'll start fixing it up for you. You know, a few touches of home. We can take over your old bedroom stuff and put in some new touches as well."

"I don't know what to say, Mom."

"Just say yes, and we'll all get to work." Beth's words were Rita's final straw. She knew God's destiny for her would take her north.

"Yes," she replied into the telephone receiver. "I'll take the train to Fairbanks when the tracks are open for the tourist season. That will be May fifteenth. Can you meet me?"

"You bet," Beth replied, not hiding the joy in her voice.

That left only one unspoken problem. Mark.

As if interpreting the silence, Beth braved a question. "Do you want me to tell Mark that you're coming home?"

Rita started to say no and then changed her mind. It would be fairer to warn Mark of her impending arrival. "Yes," she said softly. "Tell him my plans. I don't know that he cares anymore. I sent him only one letter, and he never wrote back. But, I'd still feel better if he knew."

"I understand, and I will let him know." Her mother's words offered a bit of solace.

"Mother?" Rita questioned. "Do you think he still cares for me?"

"Do you want him to?" Beth asked.

After a difficult pause, Rita spoke. "Yes, I do. I really want him to still love me."

"Then give it over to God," Beth suggested, "and trust Him for the rest."

"You're right, of course," Rita murmured. "It's really a matter of trust."

Rita was glad for the long train ride home. The miles offered her twelve hours of contemplation time before she would arrive in Fairbanks. For most of the trip, Rita rode the train in the area between cars. She opened the upper portion of the

door and allowed the chilled May air to assault her face. The cold felt good and the fresh air seemed to clear her mind.

As the scenery rushed past her, Rita found herself praying. "God, You know my heart even when I don't. This time, I feel that I truly love Mark, but I don't know if he still feels the same way about me or not. Father, I know I must leave this matter to You. Help me not to take it back and work it for my own will rather than Yours. Amen."

The ride lasted from eight in the morning until eight at night, passing through miles of Denali National Park. It even afforded Rita a picturesque glimpse of Mt. McKinley before the clouds moved in and sheltered the summit from view.

From time to time the forest gave way to glimpses of small towns. Railroads always seemed to approach towns from the backside, Rita decided. It appeared to be just the opposite of the highway on which she'd driven north a year earlier.

When she caught sight of the DEW line, America's Defense Early Warning system in case of Soviet attack, Rita knew that she was nearly to Fairbanks. She mentally calculated the plans from there. They would no doubt stay overnight, given her parents'

dislike of traveling the highways after dark. That would make it at least noon tomorrow before she'd actually make it home. How much longer after that before she could see Mark and talk to him?

When the train pulled into the station, Rita put her concerns of Mark aside and rushed to greet her parents.

"I'm so glad to see you both," Rita exclaimed, throwing herself into their arms. "It's good to be home."

"Well, nearly home," August laughed. "You don't mind staying over tonight, do you?"

Rita laughed. "No, I already had that planned. Did you get the things I sent by air express?"

"They're safe and sound in your new cabin," August replied.

"My new cabin," Rita repeated. "It seems so strange to know that I'm now a homeowner."

Beth laughed and gave Rita a squeeze. "You're going to love it. I just know it. You should have seen the way your father and Mark worked to finish it."

"Mark helped?" Rita questioned. Was that an air of hope for something more in her tone?

"Mark nearly built it himself," August

answered honestly. "I can't move like I used to. Gerald came over, and he and his older boys offered a hand as well. It was a real family affair once your mother started adding the homey touches."

"Well, well." Rita's tone made her pleasure evident. "It's going to be hard to stay over, knowing all that awaits me."

"It'll be just like Christmas," August said with a smile. "You'll have to wait until morning to unwrap your gifts."

"Like Christmas, eh?" Rita questioned teasingly. "Then we can get started at four o'clock in the morning, right?"

August and Beth rolled their eyes. "Some things never change with kids," August laughed. "Come on, we'd better get you fed and to bed if you plan to get started that early!"

Rita didn't get her parents up at four. She relished the soft mattress of the hotel bed and lingered there until her mother announced that they were going down for breakfast without Rita if she didn't get up.

She could hardly sit through breakfast while thoughts of Mark pressed her to hurry. When they were finally headed home, she couldn't help but count the landmarks and towns. Minutes seemed to drag by, while Rita barely heard the things her parents had to say.

By the time August finally pulled down the dirt road that led to the Eriksson homestead, Rita was gripping the door handle in anticipation. Home had never looked so good to her.

"I drew you a map," August said, coming to a stop beside Rita's car. "I know you want to head right over, but you could stay a spell."

"That's true," Beth added, getting out of the car. "I'd be happy to fix you lunch and —"

"Thanks anyway," Rita interrupted.

Beth and August laughed. "Go on then," August said. He put his arm around Beth and, for the very first time, Rita felt the warmth of the love they shared. She'd once questioned what her father could have possibly seen in her mother. Now, however, Rita thought she was coming to understand.

Rita glanced around, wondering if Mark was working with the dogs. Beth read her daughter's mind and shook her head.

"He's not here, Rita. He's getting your dogs settled at the new place."

Now Rita was even more motivated to see her new home. "I'll see you later," she grinned and jumped into her car.

"Don't speed," August called out to his daughter. "Remember where that got you before."

"I do," Rita said, remembering it fondly. "It found me the man I intend to marry!"

August shook his head and waved her on. It was good to know that his youngest had finally found happiness. Better yet to know that she'd finally found peace of heart and soul.

Rita glanced only briefly at the map. From her father and mother's earlier description and directions, she knew without the paper just where she was going. She crowded the speed limit as closely as she dared and finally found her turnoff just as her patience was wearing thin.

The dust sprayed out behind her car as Rita moved closer to her cabin. She rounded the final bend to face a huge banner with bright yellow letters strung across the road. As she approached the cabin, she found that banners were flying everywhere. WELCOME HOME, they read.

Across the front porch of the huge cabin, another banner in multiple colors reiterated the message. Rita felt her heart pound faster. Were the banners her parents' idea or Mark's?

Parking the car, Rita got out and stopped. She looked around her, just trying to take it all in for a moment. The clearing set out before her held not only the cabin, but a partially finished shed. From behind the house, Rita could hear the dogs raising a ruckus. They knew their mistress was finally home.

She searched the area for some sign of Mark's motorcycle or truck. Surely he hadn't tended the dogs and left. If he had, did that mean he no longer cared for Rita in the way he once had?

Rita felt a gripping despair come over her. Maybe her anticipated homecoming wasn't what she'd hoped for. Maybe Mark's kindness and work had been done out of his partnership status with her father. Maybe Mark wouldn't want to see her. After all, he'd never even acknowledged her letter.

Rita swallowed hard. Whatever happened was in God's hands. She had to trust Him and count on Him to make the way for her life. Breathing a little easier, Rita stepped forward to explore her new home.

She hadn't taken more than two steps

when the unmistakable sound of a screen door opening caught her ear. Looking up, Rita found Mark coming out of the cabin. He walked to the edge of the porch and stood at the top step.

Rita stopped and appraised him for a moment. His expression was masked from revealing whether their reunion was a welcomed one or something that he was merely tolerating. His brown eyes were serious, and Rita felt their warmth as his gaze penetrated her fears.

The wind in the trees broke her concentration and Rita turned momentarily. She looked back quickly, half expecting Mark to have moved or done something that would indicate how he felt. Instead, he said nothing, did nothing. What did it mean?

Chapter 18

Mark's words came back to haunt Rita. She remembered in Nome when he told her, "Some day you'll come to me and I'll be there with open arms just for you."

Here I am, Rita thought to herself. *Now where is the open-armed welcome that he promised?*

Mark had played his game long enough. When a grin spread across his face, he couldn't help but fulfill his promise to Rita.

Rita ran across the yard and up the steps to where Mark's open arms waited. "I've missed you so much!" she exclaimed as his arms tightened around her.

"You have no idea how hard it was for me to leave you in Anchorage and wait here," Mark replied. "Thought you might have even headed off for Texas."

"I was afraid you wouldn't care anymore," Rita said, lifting her face to Mark's. She needed to see in his eyes that her fears were unfounded.

"I told you that I'm a very patient man," Mark whispered. "Although you very nearly made me a liar. It's a good thing your dad had this cabin project in mind, or I'd have never been able to get through the weeks."

"Oh, Mark," Rita said, burying her face against his chest. "I love you and I'm so sorry for making you wait so long to hear me say it."

Mark pressed his lips to the top of Rita's head. Kissing her hair, he whispered, "The wait was worth it. All things in God's timing are worth waiting for."

Rita released Mark and stepped back. "The loneliness was incredible. I thought of you constantly and all I could imagine was that my foolishness had put you out of reach forever. I was truly afraid that I'd lost my dreams of happiness."

"You're the only dream that has ever mattered, Rita," Mark said with a grin. "And let me tell you, my time up here alone has given me an awful lot of time to perfect that dream."

Rita found Mark's sense of humor contagious. "I did some dreaming of my own," she admitted. "About a tall, broad-chested law officer, who saved my life and stole my heart. You've always been a part of my dreams, Mark. And you always will be."

"Then you'll marry me?" Mark asked for the second time.

Rita stepped forward and put her arms around his neck. "I would be most happy to marry you, Mr. Williams. Positively delighted!"

"Promise?" he said, raising a questioning brow. "You aren't going to change your mind and replace me with another Iditarod dream, are you?"

Rita laughed out loud. "Not hardly, Mr. Williams. You are caught, hook, line, and harness. No Texas or race or cowboys or frozen wilderness is gonna stop me. You're stuck with me, like it or not."

"I like it," Mark said, lowering his lips to Rita's. "I like it very much." He kissed her tenderly while Rita melted against him.

When he lifted his lips, Rita sighed. "I'm going to like this, too. I can tell."

Mark surprised her by taking her hand and pulling her with him to sit on the porch step. "This is going to be new for both of us. We've both been used to independence and we've both lived our lives without real concern for the decisions we make. Now, however, we'll have to consider each other in every choice we make."

Rita nodded. "It won't be easy to change our lifestyles overnight."

"We'll no doubt have our moments when we're not very happy with one another," Mark added.

"True," Rita replied. "But if we're honest with each other and careful to work through those times, maybe we won't have to spend too much time in strife."

"It's going to be a lot of work," Mark stated.

"You sound like you did when you were training me for the Iditarod." Rita couldn't help but laugh. She saw the amusement in Mark's eyes.

"Marriage is going to be even more work than the race," Mark answered. "And a whole lot more dangerous."

Rita questioned his words. "Just what do you mean?"

"I hear you don't cook too well," he laughed. "I might be in for some strange cuisine. Then there's mending and sewing."

"Whoa!" Rita called out. "I'm a nurse, remember? I have a job that I hope to do and I enjoy working in medicine. You have the kennel and the dogs. I don't see any reason why we can't work together and trade off on the cooking and cleaning."

Mark rubbed his chin thoughtfully. "All right," he said in a teasing tone. "I suppose that's fair enough. But, I draw the line at mending clothes. I'm no good at it. I can mend harness and rigs with the best of them, but I can't even sew on a button."

Rita laughed. "Me neither. I can stitch up wounds, though. Does that count?"

Mark put his arm around her. "Maybe your mom could sew on the buttons."

"Maybe," Rita mused, "she could give us sewing lessons."

They fell silent, enjoying the brilliant sun and the warmth that filtered down to thaw the earth.

"What about dogsledding?" Mark asked suddenly.

"What about it?" Rita questioned.

"You plan to race anymore?" Mark's question took Rita by surprise.

"It all depends," Rita replied.

"On what?" Mark asked her. Now he held the puzzled look.

"On you," Rita grinned.

"Me? What are you talking about?"

"You asked me back in Nome, What makes you think I'll let you come next year?"

Mark laughed and squeezed Rita's shoulders. "I guess I did at that. But, seriously, do you want to race again?"

Rita nodded. "I thought it was wonderful. It was everything I dreamed it would be."

"You suppose marriage will be the same way?" Mark's question caused Rita to think.

"I know it will, Mark. It's the best of all possible dreams and even my goal of racing the Iditarod will never be as great as the goal of making you a good wife."

"You'll be a good wife, Texas Rita," Mark said, dropping his arm to take her hand. "There may be other Iditarod dreams, there may even be other races, but there is only one you —"

"And one you," Rita interjected.

"And together, we'll make the dream a reality," Mark whispered. "With God, we'll work to make a good life together. A life founded on Him."

Rita covered Mark's hand with her free one. Maybe it wasn't such a bad thing to give yourself over to another person, after all. Especially when that other person was God's very best answer to all your fondest dreams.

Christmas
Dream

Chapter 1

"Would you care for anything to drink?" the dark-haired flight attendant asked Mark Williams. Her brilliant smile and honey-smooth voice caused Mark to look up with a grin.

"I'll take coffee," Mark replied and turned to his wife. "How about you, Texas Rita?" The nickname was born out of his wife's pretended desire to move to the warmth of the south and forget about Alaska.

Rita pushed back her shoulder-length black hair and shook her head. "No, I'm fine."

"Where are you headed?" the flight attendant asked Mark as though she had only him to serve.

"Fairbanks."

"What a coincidence. I live in Fairbanks."

"We live near Tok, actually," Mark told her, taking the coffee.

The woman eyed Rita as though noticing her for the first time. "Oh," was all she said before pressing on to serve the next row of passengers.

"Friendly service," Mark said with a wink at his wife.

She appeared a little too friendly as far as Rita Williams was concerned. Her marriage to Mark, now barely a month old, left her feeling very possessive of the man at her side. "She was a flirt and you know it," Rita said, pretending to read the magazine in front of her.

"Your eyes look like black diamonds when you're angry," he whispered against her ear, then nipped the lobe playfully to make sure he had her attention.

"Mark!" she squealed, without meaning to. The flight attendant glanced back to see what the commotion was, causing Rita to break into a fit of laughter. "Being married to you is so stressful," she teased. "Women are always looking you over."

"Right," Mark said, unconvinced.

"I've seen it with my own eyes," Rita replied, putting the magazine into the seat pocket. "When we were at that kennel outside of Seattle and you were browsing through the sled dog possibilities, you weren't aware of the way those two women proprietors were looking you over. I thought maybe for a minute they were going to ask to see your papers."

Mark laughed. "Yes, but I was checking out the dogs, not the women, so you have no reason to be jealous."

"Jealous! Me?" Rita tried to sound indignant. "I'm not jealous, just annoyed."

Mark reached his hand up to touch her cheek. He smelled of spicy musk and looked at her with such passionate warmth that Rita instantly felt her face grow hot. "I'm yours, Rita. Nobody else matters. No one else is of any interest," he whispered low and seductively against her ear.

Rita melted against him and sighed. This was the man she loved and had pledged to spend the rest of her life with. She mentally pictured the home that awaited them outside of Tok, Alaska. A lovely cabin built by Rita's father, August Eriksson, and Mark and decorated by Rita and her mother, Beth. A lovely home. Her home. Hers and Mark's.

"You mean the world to me, Rita," Mark said, then took a long drink of his coffee before adding, "besides, who else will help me with the dogs when it's forty below?"

"Mark!" Rita exclaimed with a sharp jab to his ribs. Coffee threatened to spill on them both, but Mark mastered the cup quickly. "What a thing to say!"

"Well, a hundred dogs take a lot of work."

Rita thought of their kennel. Her father and Mark had raised and cared for the dogs when they held a partnership in the kennel. Upon Mark's marriage to Rita, August had presented his share of the kennel to them as a wedding gift. While much appreciated by the newlyweds, August's gift demanded a great deal of attention. Sled dogs needed to be constantly worked in order to stay happy and healthy.

"I hope Daddy found someone to help him," Rita thought aloud, sobering at the thought of her aging father out working in the icy north cold.

"I'm sure he did."

"You should have let me call them," Rita said. "I'm sure other people phone home on their honeymoons. What if they needed us?"

"Rita, you have nine other brothers and sisters. If there had been an emergency, they would have had a small nation of people to call to their rescue."

"I know, and there was a time not long

ago that it wouldn't have mattered to me whether they needed me or not," Rita said, remembering her rebellious youth.

Born the youngest of ten children, Rita had struggled to feel a part of the massive brood. The age differences were so diverse, as were the lifestyles and interests of her siblings, that there was never any one thread that held them all together. True, there were the threads of Christianity and two rock-solid parents who loved their children more than life itself, but until Rita had put her life in God's hands the previous March, she'd completely ignored these valid treasures.

"So do you want to stop by the folks on our way home, or shall we go to the cabin first?"

Rita heard Mark's question above the drone of jet engines and passenger chatter, but it startled her for a moment. "We're really going to keep house together," she said.

Mark laughed. "Guess so, unless you'd like to move back in with your parents and visit on the weekends."

Rita wrapped her arms around his. "No way. I'm very possessive of what's mine, and you, Mark Williams, belong to me." She grinned up at him and met his loving gaze. "I think I would just as soon go on home and call Mom and Daddy from there."

"Christmas is really going to be different for us," he said thoughtfully.

"Definitely. I've never known a time when I cherished the thought of being in the middle of all my brothers and sisters and their kids. But this year, I do. I keep thinking that they'll all be there when we get home, and it makes me so anxious. I haven't even seen some of them in years."

"It's too bad they couldn't have all come for the wedding," Mark commented.

"Yeah," Rita agreed, "but you know, I like this better. It was a trade-off, the wedding or Christmas. But I'm glad Christmas won out. Mom and Dad aren't getting any younger, and this will be a very important celebration for them. Just imagine it, Mark: all the children you'd brought into the world gathered around you with their children and, in some cases, their children's children."

"So you want to have ten kids?" he questioned.

Rita rolled her eyes. "No, I most certainly do not. Let Mom and Dad hold that record. I just want us to have a nice size family that you can seat around one table when you go out to eat."

"We could just request big tables."

"We could just leave you at home," she teased.

He ignored her. "So what do we do first? I mean when we get home."

Rita paused a moment to consider their options. "Well, I thought it would be a lot of fun to sled out and cut our own Christmas tree."

"Naturally. The dogs will be half crazy for a run."

Rita and Mark were avid dogsled racers, and anything connected to dogs and sleds had become a major part of their lives. Even though Rita had a job in Tok at one of the local doctor's offices, she was seriously considering giving it up to help Mark with the kennel. It was either that or hire someone to work part-time.

"So then what?" Mark asked.

"We decorate the tree of course," she replied. "I thought maybe tomorrow on Christmas Eve you and I could spend a quiet, romantic evening together. We could decorate the tree, drink hot chocolate, and exchange our gifts to each other."

"Didn't you get enough of that romance stuff on our honeymoon?" He sounded annoyed, but there was a twinkle in his eye.

"I'll never get enough of that romance stuff, Mark, so you'd better just get used to the fact here and now. I expect to be —"

The annoying bong of the airline's intercom system demanded their attention. "Ladies and gentlemen, this is your captain. A medical emergency has made it necessary for us to divert to Juneau. Please assist the flight attendants by returning your trays and chairs to their upright and locked positions. We'll try to be back up and running just as soon as possible, so please be patient with us. Thank you."

"A medical emergency?" Rita questioned. "I wonder if they need any help."

Mark reached up to signal the attendant. When she appeared, looking a bit harried, Mark offered her a smile. "My wife is a registered nurse. Do you need any additional assistance?"

The woman relaxed a bit. "No, we have it under control, but thank you." She gave Rita an appreciative nod.

Thick white clouds engulfed the plane as they descended. Rita felt a bit hemmed in by the sudden loss of open skies. "Seems so cold and frightening," she whispered.

Mark glanced out the window. "We'll be through it before you know and then —"

The captain's voice again interrupted.

"The National Weather Service reports a major storm has moved into the area, leaving visibility dangerously low. Another massive system has moved down from the north, dumping two feet of new snow and ice on Fairbanks, closing the airport there. We'll try to keep you posted with any news of the situation, but for now we'll be grounded in Juneau until further notice. Attendants, please prepare the cabin for landing."

"I don't believe this!" Rita tried not to raise her voice. "Mark, we have to get home. It's nearly Christmas."

Mark quickly drained the last of his coffee. "I just hope they have a good restaurant. I'm starved."

"How can you think of food at a time like this? All of our plans are in shambles. Why can't we just fly over the storm?"

"Where are we going to land, even if they do?" Mark tried to reason.

"May I take that for you, sir?" the flight attendant asked. She was all business.

"Thanks." Mark handed her the cup and turned back to talk to Rita.

"Sir, you'll have to return your tray to its upright and locked position," the flight attendant told him before he could comfort his wife.

Doing as he was directed, Mark smiled at the woman. There was no return smile for Rita to object to, but she was concerned by the woman's preoccupied manner. Were they actually in more danger than the captain had let on? Was the medical situation just an excuse?

"Excuse me, miss," Rita said, causing the flight attendant to halt. "What's the condition of the airport at Juneau?"

The woman's gaze seemed to dart from one side of the cabin to the other, as if trying to determine whether she should answer the question.

"Yeah," an older businessman chimed in from across the aisle. "What is the condition? Am I going to be able to get a cab into town?"

"I'm sure the captain can better advise us," the flight attendant said. "I'll relay your questions to him and have him check on the airport conditions." She quickly made her way to the front of the plane, leaving Mark and Rita staring after her.

The businessman had already returned his attention to a computer printout on his lap. "It's just like I thought," he muttered. "Juneau must nearly be snowed in already."

"What?" Rita questioned, leaning across

Mark. "Do you think we're in any real danger?"

"We're twenty thousand feet in the air and planning to land in high winds on what is probably an ice-covered runway. What do you think?" the man asked gruffly.

Rita was taken aback, but Mark was angered by the man's attitude.

"There's no need to be that way with her. She asked a simple question."

The man looked up at Mark and the tightness in his expression relaxed a bit. "No, there was no need, and I do apologize. I'm not going to make it home for Christmas at this rate, and I promised this year would be different. Three kids are sitting in Fairbanks, expecting me to be there on Christmas Eve for their church program, and it'll be just one more year that business came between us. I shouldn't have taken it out on you, ma'am, and I do apologize."

Rita's heart went out to the man. "I understand. I feel the same way. My family is expecting me home for Christmas as well."

The man went back to his report with a shrug that said it all as far as Rita was concerned. They were up against something bigger than they could control.

"We should pray, Rita."

Mark's words broke through her self-pity. Together they held hands, and Mark murmured petitions to God, while Rita begged forgiveness for her selfish focus.

Chapter 2

Juneau's airport was filled with disgruntled travelers, most of whom were arguing with airport officials and demanding information about their flights.

Lugging their carry-on baggage with them, Rita and Mark found a spot to sit and discuss their situation.

"I can't stand this," Rita said, plopping down beside her husband. "It isn't fair. I had such plans."

"Just be glad we're on the ground safely and not flying around trying to navigate this weather. Look out there and tell me you wouldn't rather be here safe and sound."

Rita glanced out the window. It was impossible to see anything but white. "I'd rather be almost anywhere but here!" She crossed her arms defiantly against her chest and pouted.

"Look, I'm going to brave the crowd and see if I can learn anything about our situation," Mark said, getting to his feet. "You want me to bring you back anything?"

"No," Rita replied curtly.

Shaking his head, Mark turned and trudged toward a ticket agent.

The look on Mark's face when he returned told Rita everything she needed to know. Clearly disappointed, Mark took the seat beside her and slouched down, sticking his hands deep into his pockets. "We're not going anywhere for a good long while. This storm has no intention of letting up, and there isn't any transportation in or out of town. Too dangerous."

"So we're to just sit here? Is that it?"

"That's it. Look, Rita, I know you wanted to hear better news. So did I."

Rita shook her head. "This is our first Christmas together. I had such great plans, and now everything is ruined."

"It's not ruined," Mark protested. "So we celebrate late if need be."

Rita narrowed her eyes. "You just don't get it, do you? I've planned this for months. I've given our first Christmas celebration almost as much planning as I did our wedding."

"And a lovely wedding it was, as I recall," he added, grinning from ear to ear.

Rita knew it was his attempt to lighten her mood, but she'd have no part of it. "Don't! Don't even try to make a joke about this."

"Well, what do you suggest I do? Lose my temper like you?" Mark lowered his voice to a whisper and added, "I can't see where getting angry about it is going to get us out of here any faster. You can go up there and make a spectacle of yourself by raging at the airline personnel, but I don't think it's going to change a thing."

"You just don't care," Rita said in a voice that mingled hurt and angry accusation. "If you really cared, you wouldn't talk like that."

"Well, tell me what you want to hear, Rita, and I'll say it. But my words won't change the fact that the National Weather Service has issued winter storm warnings and we're grounded hundreds of miles short of our objective."

"It's not our objective, it's home. We can't get home, and it's almost Christmas!" Rita declared, not caring that her raised voice was attracting attention.

"Rita, calm down." Mark reached out to take hold of her hand, but she pulled away. "There is a time and place for everything.

This is neither the time, nor the place."

"I'm angry, Mark. I'm angry about this storm and the complications to my plans, but most of all I'm angry at you for not understanding how important this was to me. I thought you knew me so well."

Mark eased back in his chair and replaced his hands in his pockets. "I understand you well enough to know there isn't any reasoning with you when you're like this. You're being childish and misjudging me. I care a great deal about what's important to you, and believe me, blizzard or no blizzard, if I had a sled team at my disposal, I'd put you on it. But I don't, so you're stuck here with me and all the rest of these disappointed people, and if you'd stop feeling sorry for yourself, you'd see that everyone here is in the same position you are."

"Fine!" Rita got to her feet, grabbed her purse, and stomped off without looking back once to gauge Mark's reaction. She wanted him to come after her and assure her that everything would be all right and that her Christmas dream would still come true. But he didn't.

After stomping around the terminal for about fifteen minutes, Rita was a little calmer, but no less upset. *This isn't the way I want it to be, God.* She leaned against the wall outside the ladies' restroom and looked to the ceiling.

I had such plans and hopes, she continued. *I wanted to share this Christmas with all my family. I wanted to have a romantic Christmas Eve with Mark, just the two of us in our new home with our own tree and decorations.* Tears filled her eyes. *I won't be a cry baby about this,* she thought, putting an abrupt end to her prayer.

Glancing around her for the first time, Rita noticed other travelers. Concern and disappointment lined their faces and mirrored the hurt inside her soul. Dreams were supposed to be fun, hopeful things, not painful reminders of what you couldn't have, Rita thought. At least, that was the way she figured it should be.

"You look like you're carrying the weight of the world, deary," an aged female voice called from the right.

Rita looked over to find an elderly woman sitting not five feet away, crocheting with a huge ball of white thread. The woman's gray head remained bent over her project even as she continued. "This is a sorry time to be stranded in an airport. Do you have far to go?"

"Fairbanks, and then we were going to take a hop to Tok. How about you?"

The woman looked up and smiled. "I was headed home to Fairbanks after visiting my grandchildren in Seattle."

Rita nodded but remained fixed to her spot.

"Why don't you come sit a spell with me. I'm Abbey," the woman said and cleared off the seat beside her. "Abbey Strom."

"I'm Rita Eriks—" she paused, shook her head, and began again. "Rita Williams. I'm returning from my honeymoon, but I'm still not used to the name."

Abbey smiled again and put down her handiwork. "How wonderful! And where's your young man?"

Rita grimaced. "I'm afraid I ditched him at the other end of the terminal. We had a difference of opinion."

"Ah," Abbey said with a knowing nod. "Is this your first fight?"

Rita laughed, breaking her melancholy mood. "Good grief, no. We fight all the time. Well, not really fight. I'm just opinionated and he's, well . . . he's opinionated, too."

Abbey nodded again. "Sounds like my Herman. Goodness, but that man could argue up a storm to rival the blizzard outside. Will you forgive your young man right away or make him sweat it out?"

Rita shrugged. "I don't see anything to be gained by holding a grudge. I just wish he better understood me and why it was so important to me to be home for Christmas."

"Had big plans, did you?" Abbey picked up her crocheting and resumed her work.

"The biggest," Rita replied, surprised that she could open up so easily to this stranger. "See, this was our first Christmas, but there was more to it than that. I come from a big family. There's ten of us kids, and we span a score of years and well . . . , I've not always felt very close to any of them. In fact, until recently, I wasn't on the best of terms with my mom or dad, either."

"What changed to make things better?"

"I did. I got right with God," Rita said without thought, then quickly added, "I don't mean that to sound flippant. I really did set things right with God. It wasn't like some grandiose religious experience — I grew up in church and my folks had always taught me about the Bible. It's just that I finally came to see the truth for myself."

Rita paused to take a deep breath and

realized that Abbey was staring at her blankly. "Sorry," Rita offered. "I got a bit carried away."

Abbey chuckled. "In this day and age, we feel a little compelled to justify and explain the acceptance of Christ in our lives. Faith in God seems too insignificant a thing when held up against the video game machine and virtual reality."

Rita laughed. "Where in the world did you learn about virtual reality?"

"Grandkids. I wanted to take them shopping at a local mall. You know, Grandma stuff."

Rita nodded, although she'd never known her grandmothers.

"Anyway, they insisted I come with them to the video arcade. The next thing I know, they've got me shooting and dodging everything from alien life forms to characters from the Wild West. With entertainment like that to occupy and — if you don't mind my saying so — fry their brains, listening to Grandmother talk about God is just a little on the boring side."

"Did your husband travel with you?"

Abbey's eyes glossed over, and she put down her crocheting for a second time. "Only in spirit. He died earlier this year. This is my first Christmas without him."

"I'm so sorry. I didn't mean to bring up something unpleasant."

Abbey smiled behind her tears. "Herman, unpleasant? Never!" Her mild declaration touched Rita deeply. "My Herman was a joyful man in life, and I'll not remember him any other way. He was fun to argue with, fun to work and play with, and a blessing to love and live with." Abbey rummaged around in a bag at her feet and brought out a well-worn handkerchief. After dabbing her eyes, she drew a deep breath. "Tell me about your plans for Christmas. The plans you and your young man had."

Rita was still unnerved by her blunder about Herman. "I, well, that is," she stammered and finally stopped all together.

Abbey patted her hand. "Tell me."

Rita opened her mouth and found herself relaying every imaginable detail about the plans she'd had for the holidays. "I wanted us to dogsled out. We do that, you know? Well, of course you didn't know, but we do. Mark and I both love to dogsled, and we own over a hundred dogs."

"How interesting. I've always wanted to know more about that kind of thing, but I've never known anyone, until now, who actually operated dogs and sleds."

Rita continued. "Mark and I both love to race. That's actually how we met. My father and Mark were partners in the kennel business, and when I came home from college to race in the Iditarod, there was Mark."

"The Iditarod? You don't mean that monstrous race they have every spring? The one from Anchorage to Nome?" Abbey questioned in disbelief.

"The very same. I raced it for the first time last year, and I plan to race it again. I didn't do too bad, but Mark beat me out. In fact, he saved my life on the trail, and that was when I realized how much I needed God in my life."

Abbey was a captive audience, so Rita continued. "I got caught in a storm like this one. I lost track of my dogs and found myself stranded there without my supplies or any hope of finding them. But God and Mark were watching out for my foolish attempts at independence. Mark found me and cared for me, and I saw for the first time in my life that I was no good on my own."

" 'Two are better than one; because they have a good reward for their labour. For if they fall, the one will lift up his fellow; but woe to him that is alone when he falleth;

274

for he hath not another to help him up.' "
Abbey's voice broke, and tears fell.

"That's from Ecclesiastes," Rita said, reaching out to touch the old woman's hand. "I know those verses very well. Chapter four, verses nine and ten. Mark and I had them read at our wedding, and they are very special to me."

"They were special to us as well. I hope you'll forgive this old lady's tears. I know I'm not alone and God is watching most tenderly after me. I feel His presence even now, especially now, but sometimes it's a bit much."

Rita nodded but said nothing. She continued to hold tight to Abbey's hand, and the old woman spoke on.

"I remember one of our first Christmases. We still lived in the lower forty-eight and we'd gone to one of those tree lots to find a Christmas tree. Well, what we could afford with our meager earnings and what they had there were two entirely different things. So Herman gets the idea that we should go cut our own tree down by the lake and save the money.

"Well, if ever an operation was doomed to fail, it was this one. First we couldn't find a decent tree even remotely related to the pine family, and when we finally managed to find a pitiful example of one, Herman nearly cut his foot off trying to axe the thing."

"No!" Rita exclaimed, completely caught up in the story.

"I'm afraid the money we saved cutting our own tree went to buying Herman a new pair of boots and paying a nearby farmer to pull our car out of the ditch."

Rita grinned. "Best laid plans, eh?"

"Only we hadn't laid any at all, and that was half the trouble. When we got that scrappy tree home, we realized we had to figure out how to get it to stand up in the living room. I found a bucket, Herman filled it part way with dirt, and then we put the tree in it and filled it the rest of the way with dirt and water. Then we stood back and the thing collapsed, spilling mud all over the only rug we owned."

Rita was now laughing in earnest. "What did you do?"

"I think we finally just leaned it against the wall," Abbey said, laughing with her. "Oh, it was a sorry sight to be sure, but it was one of the very best times we had together, and I will always remember that Christmas. We didn't have much money, we'd made a mess of the tree and Herman's boots, but we were so in love.

You know, when you love someone, the little things have a way of not being quite so important."

Rita sobered and nodded. She couldn't begin to imagine what it would be like to celebrate Christmas without the man she loved more than life itself. "I think I'm just learning that lesson. I guess I owe my husband an apology."

Abbey reached down again into the bag at her feet and pulled up a white crocheted snowflake. "I've been working to make enough of these ornaments to hand out to the kids at church tomorrow night, but I want you to have one for your tree."

Rita took the gift and held it up to study. "It's beautiful, Abbey. I wish I could do things like this, but I'm afraid the only sewing I'm able to do is with a suture needle and thread. I'm a registered nurse, but that's where my sewing talents begin and end."

"I guess we both have our talents, eh?"

Rita got to her feet and tucked the snowflake carefully into her purse. "Thanks, Abbey. I think I'm going to go talk to my husband. Maybe I'll get back to introduce you two."

"I'd like that," Abbey said. "If not, I'll be praying for you."

"Me, too," Rita replied. "I mean, I'll be praying for you. I appreciate what you told me tonight. I've been a pretty hard case most all of my life, and I guess it's time for me to soften up a bit and admit I need to make some changes in my attitude."

Chapter 3

Mark felt rather proud of his ingenuity. After being told by one of the ticket agents that they'd most likely be spending the night at the airport, Mark started looking for ways to make their situation a little more comfortable. First he'd gone to the lost and found and procured from the airport personnel two long forgotten sleeping bags. They were in pretty good order and would make an overnight airport stay a lot more comfortable.

Next he'd surveyed the airport waiting areas and found a nice, out-of-the-way corner where he unrolled the bags and made himself at home. It wasn't much, and no doubt it would do very little to change Rita's attitude. He sat down with a sigh. She had a right to be disappointed, he told himself. It was just hard to imagine she couldn't see how disappointed he was, as well. Married life definitely took some getting used to. When he was a single man, an interruption of this type would have been inconvenient, but little more. It wasn't because he didn't enjoy making special holiday plans or that he couldn't appreciate coming together with family. Mark knew how important such things could be, and he knew how important this Christmas celebration was to his wife. Rita had so long been at odds with the world that now, after coming to terms with so many things, she wanted to make up for lost time. All at once.

"Ahem."

Looking up, Mark met Rita's dark apologetic eyes. With a lopsided grin, he lifted his hand to her. "Our own private utopia."

Rita tossed her purse to the ground and joined Mark on the sleeping bag pallet. "Where did you dig these up?"

Mark shrugged. "I have my ways. Like it?"

Rita nodded. "I suppose I'll like it even better in the middle of the night when I'm trying to get warm and comfortable."

"So you heard," Mark said, testing the waters.

"Of course. You know me — I asked. I thought maybe there was a chance the weather had changed in the last ten minutes and that we'd soon be on our way. You sure you don't want to get a hotel?"

"Security advised everybody to stay put. The roads are impassable, the blizzard is blinding, and the temperature has dropped twenty degrees in the last hour. I don't think we'd be wise to try it. Besides, we aren't the only plane grounded. I'm not sure the hotels can take the load. You and I are used to roughing it, though, and I figured we could sleep here a lot better than some."

"True," Rita said, sounding absent-minded. "Look, Mark, I was wrong, and I apologize. It was just so disappointing to have this all happen. I wanted things to be perfect, and now everything is out of my control and . . ." She paused, smiling broadly. "That's where it always begins, isn't it?"

"What?"

"I lose control over the situation and then I get ugly." Rita pulled the crocheted snowflake out of her purse. "I met the neatest old woman, and she gave me this. She was crocheting these for some children." Rita laughed. "Maybe my childish attitude reminded her of them — I don't know. Anyway, I don't know why, but it seemed as if I'd known her all my life. Pretty soon I was telling her everything. I mean, I just poured out my heart to her."

"Did it help?" he asked sympathetically.

Rita nodded. "It did more than that. It humbled me."

"Humbled you?"

"Yeah. There I was complaining about how I couldn't have the Christmas I wanted and how I'd made all these plans for you and me to do things together." Rita's voice dropped. "I told her it was our first Christmas."

"And what did she say?"

Rita's expression softened. "She told me this was her first Christmas without her husband. He died earlier this year. Oh, Mark," her voice cracked and she snuggled into his arms. "I felt so bad for her. The pain was so clear in her eyes, like when I'm working on a patient who's in sheer agony but who's trying hard to tolerate it. Abbey, that was the woman's name, she was so sweet. She said she was going to remember all the good times and how much fun they had together. She told me stories about their lives together, and it made me sad to think she's going to spend Christmas alone."

"Where's she going? Maybe she's spending the holidays with her kids."

"She's on her way home. She's already seen her kids in the lower forty-eight. Now she's going home to Fairbanks. I guess God used Abbey to show me how selfish I was being. I kept listening to her and thinking how lame it was for me to complain about my problems when she was facing this terrible thing. Oh, Mark," Rita said, sitting up. "I can't bear to think about losing you."

"Then don't," Mark said, pulling her tightly against him. "I'm not going anywhere. You and I will have a good long time together, and if anything happens to prove it to be otherwise, God will see us through."

"I know, but it really made me think," Rita said. "I'm disappointed by having my plans changed for a day or two, but Abbey's entire future has been rewritten. When I think of it from that perspective, I feel very childish and stupid."

"You aren't stupid, Rita."

She eased away, laughing. "But I am childish."

Mark laughed. "This is one of those questions I should answer by saying, 'Of course not.'"

"What are you talking about? One of those questions?"

"You know, like when a woman asks you if you think she looks nice. What she really wants is for you to compliment her. Or if she asks you if you think she's fat, she wants you to convince her that she looks thin."

Rita frowned in concentration. "So you think I'm fat?"

Mark's howl of laughter brought stares from other travelers. "That's exactly why I should never have answered you."

Rita shook her head. "No, really. If you think I'm fat . . ."

Mark took her face in his hands and kissed her soundly. Pulling away he whispered, "You are not fat, but yes, you do act childish at times. Now, explode and rage at me if you must."

Rita shook her head. "I'm sorry I got so angry, Mark. I should never have taken it out on you. Of course, you must be just as disappointed as I am, but I didn't think about your feelings and that was wrong. I assumed that because you were trying to handle things in a positive manner, it wasn't important to you. I guess I wanted you to tear your clothes and weep with me over the loss."

Mark breathed a sigh of relief. "I just figured getting angry about it wouldn't change things. It doesn't mean I'm not angry or that I'm not annoyed to find my plans disrupted."

"Would you like some peanuts?" the voice of a woman sounded from behind Mark.

"I beg your pardon?" Mark questioned, turning.

"The airline realizes the inconvenience to your travel plans, and we thought we'd show our regret by offering some snacks."

"I'd rather you put us in the air again," Mark said flatly.

"Or accommodate us with a hotel room," Rita added.

"Really," the attendant said defensively, "the airline isn't responsible for what happens because of the weather. We'll happily see you to your destination when the snow clears, but we can't be held accountable for things out of our control."

Mark took the offered foil packages and smiled. "I wasn't trying to blame you, personally. It is Christmas, after all, and you probably have somewhere you'd rather be as well."

The woman nodded. "That's for sure. I hate this northern route, but I have family in Fairbanks and that makes it convenient. But I do get tired of the fog, snow, and ice delaying flights and causing people to miss out on important things. They always seem to blame the first airline person they come in contact with."

"I'm sure that's true," Rita offered sympathetically. "If it's any consolation, we don't blame you."

The woman nodded and moved on, leaving Mark with the distinct impression that she'd squared her shoulders to do battle with the next traveler.

"That's not a job I'd want just now," he said, opening a package of peanuts and handing them to Rita.

"Thanks. I suppose it's a bit like nursing. People are always looking for someone to blame for their ills." She ate a couple peanuts and continued. "I remember one mother in Anchorage when I was still in training. She'd just been told her daughter had cancer and the first question out of her mouth was, 'How did this happen? Who could have given it to her?' I felt sorry for her. She just wanted someone to be responsible for the problem and solve it."

"Yeah." Mark finished a bag of nuts and opened a second. When he'd finished those as well, he started toying with the foil wrappers. "Well, one thing's for certain,

Texas Rita, we've got no one to blame but ourselves for traveling in Alaska during the winter."

"I suppose you're right. We even discussed the possibility of bad weather when we were planning the wedding. I seem to remember Mom pointing out that maybe we should come back sooner from our honeymoon to avoid the possibility of missing Christmas at home."

"Maybe one of these days we should start listening to that woman," Mark replied.

"I'm going to," Rita agreed. "She always seems to give good advice. She's the one who told me before we got married that my temper was going to get me into trouble if I didn't learn to control my mouth."

She paused. "Look, Mark, I know this isn't going to be easy for me. I'm too inclined to react to what's going on instead of thinking it through. I do love you, though. I hope you believe me and know that I will try to do better."

Mark held up his creation. It was a foil wrapper ring he'd devised. "Our love for each other is like this ring. Like the rings on our fingers. It has no beginning and no end. I know you love me, Rita. I'd never have thought it to be conditional or I'd never have married you. And just as your love isn't conditional, neither is mine. I love you with all my heart — and I knew your stubborn temper all too well when I married you. Now, I'm not saying don't work on it. I think you should. Just like I need to work on my know-it-all attitude."

Rita looked surprised and Mark laughed. "Don't tell me that little confession surprises you."

"I suppose it does. I didn't think you knew — Well, I mean . . ."

"Didn't think I knew how oppressive I could be about how to do things and when and where to do them?" Mark laughed. "How could I not? Look, these are things we can help each other through as long as we remember our love for each other."

Rita took the foil ring and put it with the crocheted snowflake. Tucking her purse safely between them, she snuggled down on the sleeping bag, and Mark immediately joined her. Wrapping her in his arms, he heard her sigh and knew that all was well.

"I love you, Mark."

"I know you do," he said, inhaling the sweet flowery fragrance of her hair. "And I love you."

"Maybe we could have a code word," Rita suggested.

"A code word?"

"Yeah, you know, a word we could say when we hear the other one starting to lose control in our problem areas."

"What kind of code word?" Mark tried hard to keep from smiling when he added, "Something like, 'Knock-It-Off'?"

Rita laughed. "Something like that, only just between you and me. Something personal to us. Hey, I've got it! 'Iditarod.'"

"Iditarod?"

"Sure. If I start to get out of control with my temper, you could just say, 'Rita, Iditarod!' Then walk away or wait for me to acknowledge what you've said. When I hear that word, I'll know that I need to rethink the way I'm acting and what I'm saying."

"And you won't get even madder because I pointed out that you were losing your temper?"

"Are you going to get mad if I point out that you're being a know-it-all?"

Mark laughed. "Probably, but I'll give it a try. Iditarod it is."

Chapter 4

Mark eased out of Rita's arms and thrust off the sleeping bag. More than a little anxious to know what the weather was doing, he didn't have to go far to realize nothing had changed. The windows were still thickly covered in ice and little light shone through.

"The storm is as strong as ever," an airport maintenance man told him. The man was decked out in heavy coveralls and a beaver cap and looked anxious to be on his way.

"There's no news at all?" Mark questioned before the man could leave.

"Only thing I know is that everything north and west of here is covered in a good three feet of new snow. The windchill is pushing minus sixty, and nothing and nobody is moving out there," the man said, gesturing to the window.

Mark watched the man exit through a doorway marked Airport Personnel Only and felt hopelessness wash through him. He'd have to go back and tell Rita that they were snowbound for at least another day. By the looks of it, they were snowbound for another night as well.

"Lord," he whispered, "I believe You have all of this under control, and as much as I'd like to be home right now and as disappointed as I am that we're stuck here on the eve of Your Son's birth celebration, I believe nothing happens by chance. If there is something here for me to learn or someone I'm to help, then open my eyes to it. Show me how to get through this thing, in Jesus' name, amen."

He glanced up to find Rita coming toward him. Her bleary-eyed expression and yawn made him wonder if she'd had a hard time sleeping.

Rita glanced first to the ice-covered window and then back to Mark. "I suppose you're going to tell me it's still snowing."

"Yup. Airport maintenance said we might as well get used to this place."

"Oh goody." The sarcasm was clear in her voice as she continued, "Maybe we could start picking out wallpaper and carpet."

Mark laughed. "Wouldn't do any good. He also told me nothing is moving out there. All of Juneau is shut down tight."

They walked arm in arm back to their things. "You got any food in those bags?" Mark asked hopefully.

"Not even a candy bar. Why don't we try the restaurant? Surely they aren't out of food yet."

"Let's get a locker then and put all this stuff inside. I'd hate to have to hunt it down in case someone decided to get greedy," Mark said, rolling up the bags.

Rita followed suit. When everything was safely stashed, Mark turned and kissed her lovingly. With wide eyes, Rita looked up in surprise. Mark kissed her nose and pulled her hand into his.

"Merry Christmas Eve," he said softly. "I only wish it could have been the way we dreamed of it."

Rita said nothing until they'd reached the restaurant. It was crowded, but they agreed to take the only table remaining — in a small corner of the smoking section. When they were finally seated and had been handed menus by a woman whose name badge read "Nell" — and whose attitude clearly showed her dismay at the weather — Rita turned to Mark with some questions.

"So if things had worked out, what plans did you have for today?"

Mark considered his answer. "Are you sure it wouldn't just make us more depressed to talk about it?"

"I want to know," she insisted. "If I can't live it in full, at least I can imagine it."

"Well, I suppose I can get into that," Mark replied. "I guess the first thing I wanted was to wake up in each other's arms."

"We did that."

"True, but I had other things in mind as well." The mischievous thoughts he had must have been reflected in his eyes, for Rita blushed attractively and lowered her eyes.

"Yes . . . well . . ." She kept her head down. "What else?"

"I guess I thought like you that we might hike out with the dogs and get a tree. Then we could build a great big fire and brew some of our special coffee blend and decorate the tree."

"Sounds identical to my dream day," Rita said, finally able to look him in the eyes again.

"Then after we made the appropriate phone calls to wish everyone a good day and finalize plans for the Christmas morning celebration, we could plan a special dinner, and I could give you an early Christmas present."

"Really?" Rita questioned. "A present? What kind of present?"

"Oh, no you don't. I'm not giving you even a hint of what it is, although . . ." He paused as if trying to decide whether to reconsider. "No, I won't do it. You have to wait."

"But you were going to give it to me on Christmas Eve, and this is Christmas Eve."

Mark laughed at her childlike persistence. "I had planned to do it in a special way. You know," he sobered, "I wanted candlelight and music."

"Well, there's something playing on the restaurant intercom," she said with a smile.

"No, Rita, and that's final." He smiled and got up. "I'm going to find a restroom. When and if the waitress makes it back, let her know I want coffee and the breakfast special."

"Yes, sir!" she exclaimed with a pout.

"Iditarod, Rita dear, Iditarod."

Rita laughed as Mark walked away. He grew more special to her with each day. She couldn't imagine what life would be like without him, nor did she want to try.

"Have you decided what you want?" demanded the irritated voice of the waitress Nell.

Rita glanced up. The woman, tall, thin, and very blonde, acted not the least bit concerned about her surly attitude. "Yes, we'll both have coffee and the breakfast special."

"How do you want the eggs?"

"Scrambled on both," Rita said, trying her best to sound sweet. Coals of kindness, her mother would have said, often turn around the sourest disposition.

"We're out of wheat bread, so you'll have to have white toast or pancakes."

"The toast is fine."

"The special comes with your choice of orange, apple, or grapefruit juice." Nell looked down at Rita, expecting an instant answer.

"Well," Rita considered the matter. "I guess we'll both take orange juice."

"We're out of orange juice."

"All right, then apple." The woman wrote furiously on the pad and started to leave.

"Oh, and if it wouldn't be too much trouble," Rita added, "I'd like some cream for my coffee." The woman glared but nodded and went off in the direction of the kitchen.

Poor woman, Rita thought. *No doubt she's missing out on a special time with her family, too.* The thought made Rita take a look around, and as if seeing the situation for the first time, she suddenly realized that all these people were missing out on something. As she studied the people at the various tables, Rita happened to notice a row of candles and holders on a shelf above the water glasses. Mark had thought of having candlelight and music for their Christmas Eve dinner. Maybe he'd enjoy it for his Christmas Eve breakfast instead.

Nell returned with the coffee and juice, wearing the same harried expression. Digging into her pocket, she produced several containers of cream and deposited them.

"I was wondering," Rita began, hoping she wasn't going to further irritate the woman.

"Yeah?" The woman stuck her pencil behind one ear and waited for Rita to speak.

"Well, I suppose in the middle of this mess, the last thing you need is someone with a special request, but," Rita paused, trying to determine how Nell was taking this approach. The woman's expression was unchanged, however, so Rita continued quickly. "Well, I noticed you have some candles over there." Rita pointed and smiled weakly. "My husband and I are newlyweds and . . . well . . . we, I mean I'd like to surprise him with a candle this morning. Could I buy one?"

Tears of pain filled Nell's eyes.

"I'm sorry, did I say something wrong?"

Nell shook her head. "No, I'm afraid this weather has gotten to me. I'm not myself, not at all. I'm sorry."

Rita put her hand out to touch Nell's arm. "I'll bet you had big plans for Christmas Eve, too."

"I sure did. But it's not going to happen now."

Rita noticed some customers not far away who were trying to catch Nell's eye. "I shouldn't have kept you so long. I see some of the other customers are waiting for you."

"Let 'em wait. You're the first person today who's showed me any kindness."

"Everyone is so focused on their own disappointments," Rita offered. "I have to admit, I wasn't feeling too kindly myself last night."

"What changed your mind?" Nell asked, suddenly seeming to need answers to unspoken questions.

"I realized that being mad about the situation wouldn't change it. I also met a wonderful old woman who reminded me to be thankful for what I had instead of mourning what I didn't."

"It's just that I was sure my boyfriend was going to propose tonight. His sister told me he'd been making plans for a big dinner out and that he'd made several trips to the jeweler's. I was sure this was it."

"I'm sorry. I know this must be very hard for you. Not only are you stuck in a place where you can't get to him, but you have to serve all these angry customers. I'll say a prayer and ask God to help you through it."

Nell's face contorted several times as though she was trying to keep from crying. "Thank you." She sniffed back her tears and hurried to where the candles were. Bringing one back, she inserted it into the holder and put it on the table.

"I don't have any matches," she said before offering Rita a smile and leaving.

Rita pulled a lighter out of her purse. Thanks to her backwoods habit of keeping the tools for starting a fire close at hand, Rita quickly had the candle lit.

"What's all this?" Mark asked, taking his seat.

"You wanted candlelight and music. I begged the waitress, and she brought it to me."

"Our waitress performed an act of generosity?"

"Oh, Mark, it's so sad. I started talking to her, and she told me how her boyfriend was supposed to propose tonight. Now she's stranded here working instead of getting a diamond."

"That is too bad, no wonder she's —"

"Two breakfast specials," Nell said, in decidedly lighter spirits. She smiled and winked at Rita. "If I can get you two anything else, just let me know."

Mark's amazement registered on his face, and Rita burst out laughing. "See where a little kindness will get you?"

"You must have given a great deal of kindness to get a smile out of that woman!"

"Iditarod, Mark Williams," Rita said with a knowing look.

"Okay, okay." Mark tried hard to sound oppressed, but he reached out and touched Rita's hand. "Let's pray." Mark blessed the food and prayed for an end to the storm before giving Rita's hand a squeeze. "The candle's a nice touch, Texas Rita."

"So do I get my present?" Rita asked

with a forkful of eggs halfway to her mouth.

"No, but you do get my undying devotion, love, and admiration."

Rita held the fork suspended in air and thought for a moment. "I suppose that will have to do," she said with a sigh and ate the eggs.

"I love you, Rita. You're something else, you know?"

"Why do you say that?"

"You changed that woman's whole day, all because you took time to extend some Christian love."

Rita blushed under Mark's scrutiny and raised her coffee mug to give a toast. "To us and the others who are stuck here. Happy Christmases for everyone . . ."

"And may they all know the real meaning of the season," Mark added.

"Amen," Rita breathed, touching her cup to Mark's.

Chapter 5

The day wore on in absolute lethargy. There was no break in the weather and no hope of getting beyond the closed confines of the airport walls. Feeling a little hemmed in, Rita went in search of something to eat, while Mark decided to stretch his legs.

"That's my ball!" one child exclaimed to another, and a tug of war ensued not three feet from where Mark stood.

"Mom! Danny won't let me have my ball."

"It's my ball. I brought it on the airplane!"

Mark chuckled to himself, but the old man sitting nearby did not. The scowl on his face and his low-pitched grumbling made it clear that the man was unhappy.

"They sure have a lot of energy," Mark commented to the man.

"They ought to be taught some manners," the stranger replied as three children ran willy-nilly past them. The argument for the coveted ball had not yet reached its peak.

"I want it!" the smallest of the three kids yelled.

"They're just excited," Mark said, laughing as the group went by in a whirlwind of colors and flailing arms.

"They're unruly and out of control," the aging man grunted.

Mark eyed him for a moment, then not knowing what else to do, extended his hand. "I'm Mark Williams."

The man eyed him suspiciously and, without accepting Mark's hand, harumphed his displeasure with the whole situation.

Mark thought the expression in the man's eyes was nearly one of pain. "I have some aspirin in my carry-on bag if you need some."

This caught the man's attention, but he shook his head. "What I need is for those young hooligans to be seen and not heard."

Mark smiled at the man's old-fashioned notions. "They are kids, and they've been confined to an airport for some time now. Besides, it's Christmas Eve. No doubt they're excited about celebrating and seeing what kind of presents are under the tree."

"That's all anyone really cares about this time of year. The greed is outrageous," the man said, drawn almost unwillingly into conversation.

"I think that's true of a lot of folks." Mark took a seat beside him and noticed the intricately carved cane at the man's side. "May I?" he asked, motioning to the cane. The man shrugged indifference, and Mark continued to speak while inspecting the object. "Oak, right?"

The man nodded.

The head of the cane was carved with a remarkable likeness of an eagle's head. "This is some beautiful work. Did you purchase it here in Alaska, Mr. . . . ?"

The man's anger seemed to abate slightly. "Bart Thomas is the name. Got it near Sitka several years ago."

"I've seen others that were similar, but none so well crafted."

The sound of a screeching child followed by a motherly reprimand caught the man's attention. "It's about time!"

"Well, Mr. Thomas, I remember being a kid at this time of year. The excitement and fun blotted out everything else. I knew the season was about the birth of Jesus, but it was a lot of fun to imagine what I was getting for Christmas and to keep secrets about what I was going to give."

The man's defensive walls seemed to go up. "They don't care about the season or what it costs their elders. They only care about getting the latest advertised gadget or whatnot."

"Seems kind of harsh to lump all kids into one package. They could just as easily lump all older people into the stereotype of being senile." Mark handed the man his cane.

"Kids these days are given too much, too soon. They expect it to just keep getting bigger and better. Why, I remember being perfectly entertained with wooden blocks at their age, but now it has to be computerized or electronic to be of interest to them."

"That is a growing problem. Especially in commercial areas. I still see a lot of simplicity in the small towns, however. Although," Mark said with a smile, "they have plenty of commercialism and name brand products there, as well."

The kids raced by again, this time intent on battling for first place to the drinking fountain.

"I beat you!" a voice cried out.

The taller of the three shoved aside the winner. "I'm oldest so I get to go first."

"Mom!"

"See what I mean? Greed. Pure and simple," Bart said, thumping his cane on the floor.

Mark eyed the balding man for a moment. He looked to be in his seventies, maybe older. Then again, maybe his negative attitude made him look older.

"Are you from Alaska, Mr. Thomas?" Mark questioned softly.

"No," the man replied, then turned steely blue eyes on Mark, "and if you're going to insist on calling me by name, then you might as well call me Bart."

"I'd like that," Mark said, extending his hand once again. This time the old man hesitantly shook it. Mark was careful not to squeeze the gnarled hand too tightly. "You can call me Mark. Are you traveling alone?"

"As usual," Bart answered, sounding bitter. "I offered to bring my youngest son, but he was too busy making the almighty dollar to take a little time off to help me out."

"Are you up here to see family?" Mark asked, trying desperately to draw the man's glowering expression from the children. They were only an arm's reach away, shoving each other and bickering about who got to play with what first.

"Go sit down with your mother and be quiet!" Bart suddenly demanded. The kids immediately fell silent and looked at Bart in surprise. The youngest broke into tears and ran to his mother's waiting arms.

Mark could see that the woman had watched the entire scene. She seemed to understand and, at Mark's apologetic expression, smiled slightly and patted the back of her crying child.

Bart thumped the cane a couple times as if it helped to calm his nerves. "Should have never made this trip. Nobody appreciates it anyway."

"Why do you say that? Wasn't your family happy to see you?"

Bart grunted. "I suppose my daughter was happy enough. She complained the whole time about her finances and how expensive it was to live in Alaska. When I told her she ought to come back to the lower forty-eight, you would have thought I'd suggested she move to Siberia."

Mark chuckled. "Sounds like she has some fire to her."

"Oh, that's nothing," Bart said, temporarily forgetting the kids, who were now racing up and down the aisle. "She quit four jobs in two months. Told me they didn't appreciate her style of doing things. In other words," Bart paused and leaned closer to Mark, "she didn't want to do what she was told. When I mentioned this possibility, she told me I didn't understand her generation. Told me I was too old to appreciate what she was up against in this day and age, especially as the wife of an air force captain who was gone more than he was home."

"She probably feels very isolated. Where does she live?"

"Fairbanks. I've never cared for the town, and I'm glad to be headed home."

"Did you just go up for Christmas?"

"Yeah, but I went early so I could be with my other three kids and their families for Christmas Day. Not that any of them will miss me now."

Mark frowned. "Why do you say that?"

Bart's expression contorted, passing through looks of anger, pain, and finally, resolve. "I'm old, and I don't have anything to offer. I don't know the latest crazes, and if I give anything other than cold hard cash for gifts, the kids just take it back and exchange it for whatever it is they want anyway. My grandkids are as greedy as their parents, and the whole lot disgusts me."

"Surely something keeps you going back?"

Bart shrugged and glared at the still-racing children. "I keep hoping something will change."

"But it doesn't?"

"Nope. I'm just an old man who isn't in tune with the times and who doesn't have anything to give that anybody wants."

"I find that difficult to believe. You seem to be quite intelligent. I'll bet you have a lifetime of stories to share," Mark commented.

"Hah! The day those hoodlums want to sit and listen to stories is the day I'll fall over dead!"

"I beg your pardon?" Mark was genuinely surprised by Bart's response.

"They don't care, I tell you." Bart thumped the cane nervously. "I've tried to share all sorts of things with them. Gave my daughter her mother's depression glass and she said, 'Well, thanks, but I don't know where I'll ever find a place for it.' Gave my son a collection of commemorative coins from the World's Fairs his mother and I had attended. We used to do that every year, you know."

Lost in his memories, Bart didn't wait for Mark's reply. "Liddy, that was my wife, wanted to see as much of the United States as possible. We went to the World's Fair celebrations, tourist attractions, museums, all the capitals — wherever she wanted to go, we went."

Mark noted the loneliness in Bart's voice. He suspected the old man wasn't nearly as angry as he was lonely and displaced. "And your wife is gone now?"

Bart nodded. "Nigh on ten years. She turned sixty and just up and died." The cane thumped twice, then fell silent. "My son said the coins could probably be sold for quite a tidy sum since we had so many consecutive issues. I got mad and told him if that's the way he felt, I'd just take them back."

Mark nodded. "They didn't hold the memories for him that they did for you, I take it?"

Bart shook his head. "Guess not. Greed, that's what holds my children's interest."

Mark was compelled to say something, but hard-pressed to figure out what it was. He could address the issue of loneliness and how the holidays were always difficult to face without the one you loved, although he was no real expert on that subject. He could imagine, remembering Rita's story about Abbey, that living without a lifetime mate was at best, difficult, and at worst, unbearably painful.

"My kids see dollar signs, and old Dad has never been with the times enough to know what's what."

"It's mine!" The boys were back, and all three were scuffling to take control of a toy car. It would have turned into an outright brawl, but Mark interceded.

"Hey, you want to take this wrestling match somewhere else?" His voice was nonthreatening, almost jovial. The boys stopped what they were doing and froze in place. "I like Christmas," Mark continued, "but I don't like fighting."

Just then the boy's harried mother came up, toting an infant on her hip. "I'm sorry," she offered Mark and Bart. "They're a real handful and well . . ." She pulled the three boys to her side.

"If you can't control them, you should make them sit with their father," Bart grumbled.

"They don't have a father," she snapped. "At least not one that wants to be a father."

Bart was clearly taken back, but he

didn't say anything. Mark tried a sympathetic approach. "Sorry. Look, they aren't being that much of a bother. I was just afraid they might get hurt."

The woman nodded, seeming to take Mark's kindness hesitantly. "I'll try to keep them out of your way." She herded the boys back to where their things were, and Mark watched as she shook her finger at them and whispered reprimands.

Bart was strangely silent for several minutes, and Mark glanced around for Rita. She had gone off to find them something to eat, and he was beginning to feel pretty hungry. Mark remembered Rita's gesture with the candles, and his heart warmed at the thought of her.

"Why are you smiling now?" Bart questioned, shaking Mark out of his thoughts. "I suppose it's more of that Christmas cheer and goodwill you're so fond of."

"I am fond of it," Mark agreed. "I love Christmas. I love what it represents and the joy it brings me."

"Commercialism is what it represents, and it brings a lot of overspending and disappointment."

"No," Mark replied seriously. "It doesn't at my house." Bart's eyes narrowed, but he said nothing and Mark went on.

"Christmas at my house is a celebration of Christ's birth. It's a season to remember that God loved us so much, He held nothing back, He gave the very best as a gift to an unworthy world. He gave us Jesus, a Savior. Christmas is a time to remember that gift, and even though I accepted Christ as my Lord and Savior some time back, I like to remember that He didn't come as an overbearing dictator, or as a demanding Father, but as a little baby. A baby who was despised by some, worshipped by others, but nevertheless, was and is the Son of God.

"Don't get me wrong," Mark added, seeing some skepticism in Bart's expression, "we still exchange gifts, but the focus isn't on what the gift is, but on the heart of the person who offers it."

"Religious mumbo-jumbo," Bart finally said.

Mark shrugged. "To some, I suppose it seems that way. But," he smiled confidently, "I know no better way to celebrate Christmas."

Bart seemed completely unreceptive, so Mark fell silent, choosing instead to offer up a prayer for the old man. He was deep in thought and prayer when a tug came on his sleeve. Mark looked down to find one of the three boys who'd so plagued Bart.

"My mama thought you might be hungry. She made these to take to my grandma's house in Seattle, but she says we might as well eat them now."

Mark took the offered homemade pretzel. It was soft and huge, and his stomach growled loudly at the thought of eating it. "Thank you, I'll just share this with my wife when she gets back." The boy beamed and held up another pretzel to Bart.

"Sorry we were so loud," he said, his expression sincere.

Bart stared uncomfortably at the boy for a moment, then took the offered pretzel. He murmured his thanks and watched the boy scamper back to his mother.

Mark wrapped his pretzel in a handkerchief and stuffed it in his pocket. He saw Rita approaching and got to his feet. "Bart, it's been nice talking to you. If you should need anything or if you just want some company, my wife and I will be over there in that corner."

Mark pointed, but Bart's eyes were focused on the mother with her little family. The old man said nothing, but something in his expression told Mark that his heart had been softened toward the entourage of children.

Plant seeds, Mark thought. Even in the icy cold of a heart that had been frozen by greed and avarice, seeds of hope and love could be scattered. By offering up a simple pretzel and an apology, a little boy had warmed the spot on which Mark's seeds had fallen. Who knew, maybe in time, the ice would thaw.

Chapter 6

"Well you certainly look pleased with yourself," Mark commented as Rita motioned him to their corner of the airport.

"I am. Look what I managed to get. Tuna salad sandwiches, potato chips, and ta-da!" She held up a can of apple juice. "I knew you were sick of soda, and this seemed a logical substitute."

"Hey, this is great. How did you manage it all?"

"Nell."

"Nell?"

"The woman in the restaurant," Rita answered, biting into her sandwich. "The variety of food is falling off, but there's still plenty of food to eat, and if you aren't too picky you can eat rather well."

Mark started to dig in, then held up the pretzel. "Look here, I have a contribution as well."

Rita smiled and broke off a piece of the twisted bread. "Ummm," was all she muttered before stuffing it in her mouth.

The ear-splitting cry of a child in pain brought both Rita and Mark to their feet. Trained eyes darted back and forth trying to size up the emergency. Rita's short career as a nurse made her ready to spring into action, and by nature of her training, she was already cleaning off her hands and looking for how she might help.

Mark caught sight of the child and pointed as he grabbed Rita's hand and pulled her along with him. The boy was the same one who had offered him the pretzel. The worried mother had placed her infant on a blanket on the floor and instructed the other two boys to watch the baby while she tended her bleeding child.

"I'm a nurse. Can I help?" Rita asked softly, taking hold of the boy's arm without waiting for an answer from his mother.

"He fell!" The woman's voice was raised in near hysteria. "They were running. I told them not to, but they are just kids."

"Yes, and active kids will have accidents. What's your name, son?" Rita questioned the boy as she took him from his mother's arms and placed him in the chair beside her.

"His name is Timmy," the woman sobbed, and Mark put his arm around her.

"It'll be all right," he offered. "My wife is one great nurse!"

"You're a real nurse?" the woman questioned.

"Yes." Rita examined the bleeding head wound and wiped at the blood with a crisp, clean handkerchief that someone offered. "The cut isn't all that deep, but it is a bleeder." She placed direct pressure on the wound and turned to the mother. "I think he'll be just fine in a little bit. He won't need stitches or anything so traumatic. You will, however, Mr. Timmy, need to sit still for a while and take it easy. Do you have a coloring book or something to read?"

The boy nodded tearfully while his brothers stared up in awe from where they held vigil over their baby sister.

"Is Timmy's brains gonna come out?" the youngest asked, and even their mother laughed.

"If they did, Timmy wouldn't miss them," she rebuked. "If you'd been using your brains, you might have thought to mind what I said and not run up and down this terminal."

"I'm sorry, Mama," the bleeding boy said earnestly. "I'll be good. I promise."

"Oh baby, you are good. You just did a naughty thing," his mother said with tears in her eyes.

Rita pulled the cloth away and grimaced. "Mark, this bleeding isn't even slowing."

"What can we do?" the worried mother questioned before Mark could answer.

"Well," Rita said and smiled up at her husband, "I have an old herbal remedy my mother taught me. Are you game?"

"Of course, if it will help Timmy."

By now a circle of the curious had gathered, and Rita was beginning to feel rather hemmed in. "First, it would be nice if everyone would step back or go back to what they were doing. We're a bit crowded here. Then Mark, if you would go find Nell in the restaurant and ask her for some cayenne pepper." Mark nodded and went off in the direction of the eatery.

"Cayenne pepper? Whatever will you do with that?" one woman questioned from the crowd.

By this time, Bart Thomas had managed to put himself beside the still crying Timmy. "Cayenne is an old pioneer trick for stopping the blood flow. I know it works because my pappy used it when he came up here during the gold rush."

"That's right," Rita confirmed. "A few

grains, and I mean only a few — otherwise it burns the wound — will stop the heaviest flow. People even use it for internal bleeding when they're in the middle of nowhere and can't get to help. Like on the Iditarod."

"You know about the Iditarod?" Timmy questioned suddenly. "I love the dogsled races."

His mother laughed behind her tears. "That he does. It's all he talks about. He wants to ride on a sled some day and lead his own team."

"Well," Rita laughed, "it just so happens that my husband, Mark, and I raced in the Iditarod last year. We raise dogs and race whenever we can."

"You do?" the boy enthusiastically cried out, forgetting his plight. "Tell me about the race. How cold was it and how far did you go?"

"I made the full race," Rita replied, ignoring the way the circle of people pressed back in to hear her tale. "I came in seventeenth, but one of these days I'm going to win it."

"What was it like?" Timmy asked.

"Cold, tiring, and . . ." She paused, looking into the faces of the crowd. "Wonderful!"

Smiles greeted her, along with knowing nods. Soon she found herself telling the story of her race to Nome from Anchorage. She told how the race commemorated the old mail trails through Alaska during a time when there were no roads and the mail had to be mushed through on sleds. It was also symbolic, she told them, of the desperate race to take diphtheria serum to Nome earlier in the century when an epidemic had threatened thousands.

"Even though they took the serum by train from Anchorage to Nenana," she told Timmy and the attentive audience, "most folks think the Iditarod is only in memory of that race to heal folks."

Mark returned with the cayenne. Nell hurried along right behind him.

"Is the little boy okay?" Nell questioned as Rita instructed Mark to sprinkle a bit on Timmy's wound.

"He's fine," Rita said, then turned her attention back to the boy. "Just a few grains, Mark." She knew Mark was well acquainted with this method to stop bleeding, so she relaxed her grip on Timmy and watched the wound cautiously.

Mark barely dotted the cut with pepper and waited for Rita to let him know if it was enough. Everyone held their breath, and when the flow of blood seemed to miraculously stop, a cheer went up in unison.

"Praise be to God!" the mother cried out and several "amens" echoed from the crowd.

Just then an airport worker came up with a first-aid kit in hand. "Will this help?" he asked, and Rita nodded enthusiastically.

"Exactly what I needed."

She rummaged around in the metal box and pulled out sterile gauze, peroxide, antibiotic ointment, and tape. "Now if I can just find some . . . ah, here they are." She held up a small strip of unrecognizable paper. "Butterfly closures. This will hold the wound together and act like stitches."

"Stitches!" Timmy cried out, but Rita patted him reassuringly.

"Like stitches but without any needles." The boy relaxed and let Rita go to work.

"Is he up to date on his shots?" Rita questioned his mother while she worked. "You know, tetanus and such?"

"Oh, yes. I'm very careful about such things," the mother replied.

"Good." Rita had Mark tear strips of tape while she cleaned around the wound with peroxide. Seeing that this caused it to start bleeding again, Rita reused the cayenne, then smiled up at Nell. "Thanks for the help."

Nell beamed, happy to have been of use to someone.

Timmy started fussing and fidgeting when Rita took too long, so Bart took it upon himself to start telling the boy a story of when his father had panned for gold in Dawson, hoping to find enough gold to fill his boots before going home.

"Did he really find a nugget as big as his shoe?" Timmy asked.

Bart chuckled. "Naw. He did find my mother, though." The crowd laughed and began to disperse a bit. "My mother was a native to the Yukon. She was very beautiful, and she knew a bit about gold."

Timmy's eyes were wide with wonderment, and Rita finished her bandaging task without further complications. Standing to join Mark, she left the boy completely engulfed in Bart's tales of the wild Yukon and dark, frozen nights of eerie mystery.

"That old man is great!" Rita exclaimed as they went back to their corner.

"He sure is. You couldn't tell by watching him now, but just fifteen minutes ago he was cursing those kids."

"You're kidding, right?"

"Not at all," Mark watched the man, and

Rita's gaze followed his. "He was a lonely old man, hurt by some things done to him in the past — things that made Christmas seem humbug and unpleasant. Now I think things will be different for him."

"Why do you say that?" Rita asked, watching her husband with tender love. His dark eyes were fairly shining, and the smile on his face held a mystery that she wanted to understand.

"Oh, I'll tell you later tonight when we're all snuggled down and you need a bedtime story," he teased, pulling her into his arms. "You did a good thing there, Texas Rita."

She accepted his kiss with abandonment, wrapping her arms around her husband's neck. Never mind that they were in the middle of the Juneau airport. Never mind that it was Christmas Eve and they should have been home. They were together, and that was all that mattered.

Chapter 7

"The weather advisory is for all non-emergency personnel to stay off the streets," the television news anchor stated seriously. Rita and Mark stood with half of the people stranded in the airport, watching and waiting for some sign that the blizzard would abate.

"Looks like we were lucky to set down when we did," one woman in the crowd said to her companion.

"Yeah, did you hear them say there's three feet of new snow in Anchorage?" someone else commented.

"I heard them say Fairbanks is completely buried and has a temperature of minus fifty."

The crowd was alive with speculation and rumors. Rita leaned close to Mark and whispered. "Fifty below? Kid's play. Harness up the dogs, and I'll take it on."

Mark chuckled and pulled her closer. "Harness your own dogs at fifty below. I may be gallant and a wonderful husband, but I think a warm bed, crackling fire, and a hot cup of soup sound better."

"Who said you were a wonderful husband?" Rita teased, poking him playfully in the ribs.

Mark eyed her with a raised brow and a bit of a smirk. "As I recall, you did."

Rita felt herself grow flush under his impassioned stare. He was a wonderful husband. Attentive, loving, giving, but also hotheaded and know-it-all when he wanted to be. She thought to tease him with some smart retort but instead leaned up to kiss his cheek.

"Yes, you are a wonderful husband, and I wouldn't trade you for the best sled dogs in Alaska."

Mark laughed and hugged his wife. The crowd was dispersing to various corners of the terminal. Retrieving their things from the locker, Rita was beginning to feel a bit like a turtle carrying her home on her back. It seemed like the terminal grew smaller by the hour, but she knew it must just be her imagination. When enough of a path had been cleared between her and the windows, Rita purposefully wandered over and stared out through the icy covering.

Mark was instantly behind her, pulling her pack off and putting it on the floor beside his own things before wrapping his arms around Rita. She eased back against his chest and let him envelop her with his warmth.

"I tried to call home again, but all the lines are either busy or down," Mark said softly against her ear.

"I hope they aren't too worried," Rita replied. "I know how my mother can fret about little things."

"Little things like jumbo jets crashing in blizzards or skidding into the ocean off icy runways?"

"Okay, okay. I get your point," Rita said, grinning up over her shoulder. Mark squeezed her more tightly to him. "Still, I wish we could reassure them," she continued. "I know they care, and now with it being Christmas Eve and all the family except us gathered together, they'll be —"

"They'll be offering up prayers on our behalf. We're probably so covered in prayer right now," Mark said lightly, "that we'll be blessed and protected for years to come."

Rita chuckled and shifted in his arms to face him. "Oh Mark, I know we're all right, but just look at all these people. Some of them are really hurting. And some of them are completely alone."

"Like Bart." Mark's gaze traveled to where the old man sat alone.

"And Abbey," Rita said, nodding toward where the old woman worked with her crochet hook. Suddenly an idea came to her. "Mark!"

He looked down at her with a bit of a surprised expression.

"Let's get them all together and have our own celebration. All the people we ran into could use a good party. We could get Abbey, Bart, Nell, and that sweet mother with her children."

"Might just as well include anybody else who wants to participate," Mark suggested.

"Sure. We can give each person a task. I'll go talk to Abbey right now. You talk to Bart, and we'll go together to see the woman with her kids. I need to check on Timmy's head anyway. After we've decided on a time and place, I'll find Nell and see what we can do about refreshments."

Some time later, Rita came to find Mark and relate the positive reaction she'd received from Nell. "She told me she can bring us some cookies and hot cocoa. Isn't that perfect?"

"You'll have the whole terminal wanting to celebrate with us." Mark laughed and gave her a quick peck on the cheek. "You did good, sweetheart."

Rita beamed and began rummaging in her purse. "Timmy is doing great. He doesn't even have a headache. Elaine, that's Timmy's mom, told me he has an iron constitution and always has." Pulling out a small travel Bible, Rita thrust it at Mark. "I thought it would be nice if you read the Christmas story out of Luke. You know, kind of dramatic-like and with plenty of feeling."

Mark pushed back the Bible. "I don't need it. I memorized it when I was six. My grandmother paid me five dollars, which in those days was a mint, to memorize the entire second chapter of Luke. She said it was important to know about the birth of our Savior."

Rita put the Bible back in her purse. "I'm going to lead them in some Christmas songs. Oh, Mark, this is going to be great!"

"No one felt midnight was too late to celebrate?" he asked seriously. Both he and Rita had thought midnight to be a rather special time.

"Not at all," she answered. "It is

Christmas, after all. So at the stroke of midnight, we'll gather over there," she pointed and eased back against the wall.

Mark joined her with a sigh. "It seems strange not to be rushing around for last-minute preparations."

"It's wonderful. I never thought about it before, but even in the days when I wasn't focused on Christ at Christmas, I was always hurrying through the season. There were gifts to buy and decorating and trees and such. My college roommate was real big on the party aspect of Christmas, and we must have celebrated every night for two or three weeks."

"The twelve days of Christmas, eh?"

"More like the thirty-one days of December," she said, laughing. "You don't even want to know about New Year's Eve."

"I think New Year's is a great time. Renewal, reflection, restoration, and rebuilding."

"With our group it was the party scene all the way. There was no stopping to renew or reflect. That would have forced us to see how empty our lives were. I wasn't the only person brought up in a Christian home who was ignoring God's truth. There were several of us. It was probably what attracted us to each other.

We were just this side of being able to throw off our spiritual understanding and give in to wild abandonment."

Rita paused thoughtfully. "We drew unspoken, unwritten lines of agreement, however. No drinking, no smoking, no sex. We all knew the truth of God's Word and will for us; we just hoped it would be something we could put off until we were old and frumpy and had nothing else to live for."

Mark nodded. "I know a lot of folks who feel that way. Kind of deathbed Christians, if you would."

"Why is it so hard to see the immediate rewards of trusting in Christ as our Savior? Why does it take getting hit over the head by some folks in order to see what a precious gift we're wasting?"

"I don't honestly know, Rita." Mark scooted closer and pulled her against him. "Maybe it's like being snow-blind. The light is so intense that we can no longer see. The brilliance of it is blinding, so instead of basking in the warmth, feeling completely surrounded by the purity of it, we avoid it, turn away, look for something dark to hold up against it."

Rita drew a deep breath and sighed. "The light can be pretty intimidating when you're the example of darkness held up to it."

"Yeah," Mark agreed. "I know."

At midnight, Rita and Mark joined Abbey and the others for their private celebration. There was a small amount of hubbub going on throughout the terminal, but for the most part, things had quieted down for the night.

The kids were quite excited about what was to take place, and Timmy immediately chose to sit by Bart, who had become a grandfather figure to the boy.

"I thought we might sing some Christmas songs," Rita announced. "We all know certain songs from school or church. Does everyone know 'Away in a Manger'?" Everyone nodded, so Rita began the song.

The kids seemed extremely pleased to be able to participate, and after the song had finished, Timmy piped up, "We sang that song in our church Christmas pageant!"

"Yeah," one of his brothers added, "we had to recite a poem and everything."

"But we got candy after it was over," the last one added, not to be outdone.

"That's wonderful," Rita commented. "You can help with our celebration by reciting for us tonight." The boys suddenly seemed a bit shy, so Rita quickly hurried on. "You know, that song is probably one of the first Christmas songs we learn. And there's a little story I thought I'd tell that goes along with the idea of the manger scene." All eyes brightened and turned to her for the tale.

"A long time ago, a man named St. Francis was worried that common people like you and me might have trouble understanding the sweetness of Christmas. People always heard the routine message, 'Jesus was born to save our souls,'" she said in a deep, austere voice. With a smile, she softened. "Which of course He was, but in the year 1223 with so much hardship around them and not much to help them along their way, people thought of God and heaven as a faraway kind of thing."

The kids were captivated, and even Mark appeared surprised by this turn of events.

"Anyway," Rita continued, "St. Francis wanted to do something that would help the people keep Christmas in their hearts and minds. He wanted to give them something to remember, and realized that words, no matter how wondrous or special, would soon be forgotten. You see, there were no Bibles for the common people, and even if there had been, most folks couldn't read. St. Francis knew that sayings and teachings from the church were things that most people soon forgot, except when threatened with their very lives for not remembering.

"St. Francis thought and thought on this matter and decided it might be nice to dramatize the Christmas story. He found a manger and brought it into the church. This was in Graecia, Italy, and he knew everybody in town would be in church on Christmas Eve for the special services to celebrate Christ's birth. He filled the manger with straw, wrapped a bundle to look like a baby, and placed it in the manger, then had some of the church workers dress as Mary and Joseph.

"When the townspeople came to church that night, they found the nativity scene at the front of their church. It made them cry for joy because they felt they were actually a part of the birth of Jesus. Since then, people have found it comforting to have the nativity as part of their Christmas celebration. And we should remember that we are much like Mary and Joseph on that special night so long ago. We are travelers, and there is no place for us to stay. We are bedded down here at the airport without even a pillow for our heads, but God is watching over us and He sees our need."

The children's eyes were wide with wonder, and Rita noticed Abbey wiping tears from her eyes. Bart seemed strangely silent, but his face radiated a tranquility that had not been there earlier.

"I think now would be a good time for your poem, boys," Rita said to the children. Timmy motioned his brothers, Mike and Danny, to stand with him.

"I have a special Christmas gift that might be hard to see," Timmy began. "But if you listen closely, you'll hear what it might be."

Mike took his place, looking sober and thoughtful. "It isn't wrapped in paper with tinsel, tape, or bow." He paused and looked at his mother, who was mouthing the words along with him for encouragement. "But it's a gift which everyone really ought to know."

Danny stepped forward, grinned broadly at Rita and then at the rest of the audience around him. "The gift," he shouted in his best four-year-old voice, "is something special, sent from God above. The gift He gave is Jesus —" Danny's special emphasis on the word Jesus made everyone chuckle. "From God to us with love!"

Everyone cheered and clapped. The

three boys bowed several times and smiled proudly. Elaine hugged them all, while their baby sister slept soundly.

"That was perfectly wonderful," Rita said, clapping every bit as loudly as their mother.

"It's my turn," Abbey announced. She held up crocheted snowflakes. "These are for you boys and your sister, and here's one for you, Mr. Thomas." She handed old Bart the snowflake and turned to give each of the boys theirs. Only Rita saw Bart wipe a single tear from his eye and tuck the snowflake lovingly between the pages of the book he held.

"Now, I will share something else with you. My grandmother came to America from Denmark. That's very far away," she said for the boys' benefit. "In that country they speak a different language, but they still love Jesus and they still celebrate Christmas. My grandmother taught me a song, and I thought I would share it with you for our celebration."

"Oh, yes! Please!" the small group exclaimed in unison.

"It's called, 'Her Kommer Dine Arme Smaa.' "

"That sounds funny," Timmy said with a giggle.

Abbey smiled. "The English name is, 'Thy Little Ones, Dear Lord, Are We,' and it was written in 1732 by a great Danish hymn writer named Hans Brorson. When he published it, the song appeared in a book called *A Little Hymn For Children*, and with it was the Bible verse Matthew 21:16: 'Have ye never read, Out of the mouth of babes and sucklings thou has perfected praise?' "

Abbey ruffled Danny's hair gently. "Brorson wrote a great many hymns, and he is very well loved in my grandmother's country."

"Please sing it for us, Abbey," Rita encouraged and stepped back to find herself wrapped in Mark's arms. She relished the feeling of security and love.

" 'Her kommer dine arme smaa, O Jesus, i din stald at gaa; Oplys enhver i sjael og sind, At finde veien til dig ind!' " Abbey sang, then laughing aloud at the puzzled expression on the faces of the boys, she repeated the verse in English. " 'Thy little ones, dear Lord, are we, And come Thy lowly bed to see; Enlighten every soul and mind, That we the way to Thee may find.' "

"Amen," Mark said softly against Rita's ear.

"Amen," Rita echoed.

"That was so cool!" Timmy exclaimed. "I never heard someone sing in that language."

Abbey was pleased with her contribution. "Merry Christmas to you all, and may you find the Christ child in your heart always."

Nell appeared with refreshments, and after everyone was seated with cookies and cocoa in hand, Mark left Rita's side for his part of the celebration. Rita's eyes grew moist as she watched him. Her heart swelled with pride at the commanding figure he made. How different things were from just a year ago! She hadn't even liked Mark, much less loved him. Well, maybe she liked him just a little, she mused.

"I'll share with you from the second chapter of Luke," Mark commented, "and retell the story of our Lord's birth." He cleared his voice and began, " 'And it came to pass in those days . . .' "

Rita heard the words she'd heard a hundred times before. How many Christmases had those special verses been quoted, only to have Rita ignore them. She'd done a great deal of ignoring in her life. She'd ignored the love her parents had offered her and the friendship of others. She'd ignored the wonderful security of a family and home. She'd ignored God, too, only He refused to take it as well as the others had.

" 'And so it was, that, while they were there, the days were accomplished that she should be delivered. And she brought forth her firstborn son, and wrapped him in swaddling clothes, and laid him in a manger; because there was no room for them in the inn.' "

No room in the inn and no room in the hearts of man, Rita thought. Mark's tender baritone rang out, and glancing around her, Rita could see that others had gathered to listen. Perhaps they, too, had ignored the baby who had come so long ago to save them. Perhaps they were even now searching for some tiny spot in which to let the Savior take rest.

" 'And the angel said unto them, Fear not: for, behold, I bring you good tidings of great joy, which shall be to all people.' "

Rita saw the children completely taken in by Mark's animated recitation. They were his captive audience, as were the others: Nell, Bart, Abbey, and Elaine with her tiny daughter — all were immersed in this unplanned airport celebration.

" 'And suddenly there was with the angel a multitude of the heavenly host praising God, and saying —' "

Bart's gravelly voice inserted, " 'Glory to God in the highest, and on earth peace, good will toward men.' "

Everyone fell silent, but Mark nodded to Bart and the old man smiled in such a way that Rita was sure he'd finally found something very precious. Mark walked back to where Rita had taken a seat.

"You know," Elaine said softly, "I was actually dreading this holiday. I had so much anger inside me. Resentment, bitterness — you name it. I just want you all to know that this night has changed me." Her eyes reflected the truth of her statement.

"Me, too," Abbey said with a glance to Rita. "I know for sure that I never have to be alone. No matter where I am, God is there, and if I'm with His people, I have my family around me."

Nell sobbed softly and tried to hide her sniffling behind sips of cocoa, while Bart opened and shut the book in his hand to look at the snowflake Abbey had given him. Even the boys' eyes remained quietly fixed on their goodies.

The airport terminal was strangely silent, but in the distance, almost unheard, a single voice began to sing "Silent Night." Then another voice joined in. Then ten.

Then twenty, and soon, everyone was singing the haunting melody.

"Sleep in heavenly peace, Sleep in heavenly peace."

The chorus faded, and everyone nodded knowingly to one another. Mark and Rita made their way to their pallet, while Elaine bedded down with her children, kissing each one lovingly and holding them for what seemed an extra long time. When she took the baby into her arms, Rita was reminded of Mary and the wonder of that night so long ago.

"Maybe that will be us next year," Mark whispered, pulling Rita into his arms.

"I'd like that very much, Mr. Williams," she murmured against his lips. "You know," she said, pulling away and surprising him, "I really do love you."

Mark laughed. "Just now figuring that out?"

Rita sat down and motioned him to do the same. She pulled the sleeping bag over their legs and leaned back against the wall and Mark's comfortable shoulder. Sighing deeply, she sought the right words.

"It's just that I'm overwhelmed with how much God must have loved us, still loves us," she said softly. "And I'm overwhelmed at how much I love you and how wrong I was to suggest we couldn't have a fantastic Christmas, even if it wasn't the one I had planned."

She sat up and searched Mark's brown eyes. What she saw reflected was the unconditional love she'd come to count on, but there was something else as well. Could it be admiration?

"Christmas is a matter of heart," she said and reached out her hand to touch Mark's bristly cheek. "It doesn't matter where you celebrate or if there's a tree or gifts. It only matters that you see the real meaning. It only matters that you understand that Christmas is all about love. God's love for us, our love for Him and each other, and love for those yet to cross our paths who are lonely and rejected for whatever reason.

"It's understanding that God gave us the very best He had, and even though we didn't understand the sacrifice and could hardly appreciate His love, He gave it anyway because He knew without it, we would die — lonely and rejected."

Mark pulled her back into his arms and kissed her forehead. "You're quite a woman, Texas Rita. I'm glad I married you, and I wouldn't have missed this part of our honeymoon for anything in the world. There will always be celebrations with our family at home, but this family of strangers will probably never again cross our paths. We made a difference here today. I know it and feel it, just as surely as I feel your love for me."

"The real gift is that God has opened our hearts and minds," Rita said, lifting her face to his. "The real gift is understanding that He never meant for us to be lonely or separated from Him."

Mark kissed her with the same enthusiastic passion that had thrilled her a hundred times before. But this time there was something more, Rita thought. This time there was a bond of spiritual understanding that they'd not soon forget.

Sliding down to the floor of the airport, Mark pulled the bag close around them. "Merry Christmas, Rita," he whispered, his breath warm and sweet against her cheek.

"Merry Christmas," she replied. "And sweet dreams."

"Christmas dreams," Mark murmured sleepily. Neither one noticed that outside the snow had stopped and the wind had calmed. Beyond the icy windows of the airport, the north star shone brightly and pointed the way home.

The employees of Thorndike Press hope you have enjoyed this Large Print book. All our Thorndike and Wheeler Large Print titles are designed for easy reading, and all our books are made to last. Other Thorndike Press Large Print books are available at your library, through selected bookstores, or directly from us.

For information about titles, please call:

(800) 223-1244

or visit our Web site at:

www.gale.com/thorndike
www.gale.com/wheeler

To share your comments, please write:

Publisher
Thorndike Press
295 Kennedy Memorial Drive
Waterville, ME   04901